THREE AGAINST
THE TIDE

YEARLING BOOKS are designed especially to entertain and enlighten young people. Patricia Reilly Giff, consultant to this series, received her bachelor's degree from Marymount College and a master's degree in history from St. John's University. She holds a Professional Diploma in Reading and a Doctorate of Humane Letters from Hofstra University. She was a teacher and reading consultant for many years, and is the author of numerous books for young readers.

THREE AGAINST
THE TIDE

D. Anne Love

A Yearling Book

Published by
Dell Yearling
an imprint of
Random House Children's Books
a division of Random House, Inc
1540 Broadway
New York, New York 10036

Visit us on the Web! www.randomhouse.com/kids

Educators and librarians, for a variety of teaching tools, visit us at
www.randomhouse.com/teachers

ISBN: 0-440-41634-5

Reprinted by arrangement with Holiday House

Printed in the United States of America

July 2000

10 9 8 7 6 5 4 3 2

OPM

For Regina Griffin
who sees angels in the marble

Contents

THREE AGAINST
THE TIDE

Chapter One

The Visitor

IF YOU ASK PEOPLE in Charleston when the war began, they will tell you about a springtime morning when ladies cheered from rooftops and cannon fire thundered. For me it began on a Sunday in late October, when everything around me—the house, the fields, the patient river—slept peacefully in a golden haze.

Until an unexpected visitor broke the stillness of that afternoon, Terrapin Island had seemed a quiet, separate kingdom, and the cruel crusade that had begun six months before nothing more than a fleeting cloud on the distant horizon.

Papa was in his study reading. Neddie and Sammy were fishing in the tidal creek that curled through the woods behind our house. From my window I could see their heads bobbing in the tall grasses, Neddie's dark as a raven's wing, Sammy's the brownish gold of a rice field at harvesttime.

Sammy's laughter rang through the trees. I put down

my pen. I dearly missed fishing with my brothers, but my twelfth birthday had passed and Papa said it was time to learn to be a lady. That meant wearing miles of petticoats and scratchy lace collars. It meant writing in a journal every day, whether or not I had anything to say. It seemed a tragic waste of a perfect afternoon to be sitting alone writing out the particulars of my day, especially when the fish were biting. But Papa was determined to bring me up in a manner befitting a girl of my station, and I was determined to please Papa.

"Susanna! Papa! Somebody's coming!" That was Neddie.

Happy for any reason to abandon my journal, I stepped on to the second-floor piazza that wrapped around our house. From there I could see our long avenue, shaded with oak trees, and beyond it the silvery gleam of the river. A stranger on a black horse charged onto the road, raising a cloud of dust in his wake.

I went downstairs to the parlor, wondering who could be calling on us so soon. We had returned to Terrapin Island from our house in town on Tuesday last and weren't yet ready to receive visitors.

Papa came out of his study carrying his book, his spectacles perched on the end of his nose. "Susanna, what's Neddie yelling about?"

Before I could answer, Neddie burst through the door, Sammy at his heels. "Papa! There's a man coming. He's a general or something."

"He'd better not be a Yankee general," Sammy said. "I'll shoot him like this." Lifting both his arms, he pretended to aim a musket. "Pow! Right between the eyes!"

"Samuel," Papa said, frowning, "you must never speak about a man's life that way. This war is a terrible thing. Now go tell Sipsy to set another place. We have a guest."

The rider galloped into the yard and dismounted. Joseph, one of our grooms, came to lead the horse away. Brushing the dust from his uniform, the rider said, "Are you Doc Simons?"

"I am. And who are you, sir?"

"Captain Jonas Trimble's the name. From Colonel Martin's cavalry."

"What brings you to Oakwood, Captain Trimble?" Papa rested one hand on my shoulder, the other on Neddie's.

"A message from General Lee himself." Then he said, "But it ain't something that ought to be discussed in front of children."

"Can it wait a bit?" Papa said pleasantly. "The next ferry isn't for a couple of hours yet, and we're just about to have our dinner. Will you join us?"

"Oh, I wouldn't want to put you to any trouble."

"Not at all," Papa said. "We'd be honored."

For Papa, hospitality was as important as religion.

"Well, if you're sure," Captain Trimble said. "I could use a hot meal, and that's the honest truth. Living on corn dodgers is no life for anybody, I can tell you that."

Papa and I led the way to the dining room. Sipsy, our cook, brought out soup and corn bread and plates of corn and ham and potatoes. She set a basket of fruit and a cake with thick white icing in the middle of the table.

While we ate, Captain Trimble told us how he hoped to have a plantation as fine as Oakwood someday. "How many acres you got here? If you don't mind my asking."

Neddie's eyes went wide. Even he understood what an impolite question it was. But we shouldn't have been surprised. Since the beginning of the war, all manner of men had rushed to join the army. Not all of them were gentlemen. Yet Papa was not one to embarrass a guest. "Almost two thousand," he answered, picking up his coffee cup. "Mostly in rice and cotton. And we have cattle."

"Two thousand acres! It must take a trainload of workers to keep it all going."

"Indeed," Papa said. "That's why our labor supply must be preserved. The Northerners don't understand how important it is for us."

"Now there's a truth! They preach to us that slavery is wrong, but they wouldn't last ten minutes without our rice and cotton."

Just then Sipsy glided in, carrying the milk pitcher and my mother's silver coffeepot on a tray. She poured more coffee for Papa and our visitor and more milk for the boys and me.

Captain Trimble said to Papa, "Where's your missus today? If you don't mind my asking."

From across the table Neddie stared at me as if to say, "Another impossibly rude question!"

Papa's gaze slid to the portrait of our mother that hung above the fireplace. "We lost her four years ago last February. I don't know how I'd have managed all this time without Susanna."

"Fine looking woman. What happened to her?"

Sammy spoke up. "She died when the twins were born. They died, too."

At least Captain Trimble had the grace to look embarrassed. He cleared his throat and said to me, "Why, you ain't no bigger than a minute. How old are you?"

As if my age were any of his concern! But I said, "Almost thirteen."

"And wise beyond her years," Papa said.

"That must be some job," Captain Trimble said. "Taking care of this big house and two young boys to boot."

"I'm not young," Neddie declared. "I'm eleven. I don't need anyone to take care of me."

"Me neither," Sammy said. "I'm rough and tough and strong as an ox."

Captain Trimble laughed. "You look pretty strong, all right."

After we finished our cake, Neddie put down his fork and said, "Captain, what does General Lee want with our papa?"

Leaning back in his chair, the captain said to Papa, "May I talk with them present?"

"Go ahead."

"Well then. General Lee is on his way to Charleston," the captain began, "to organize our troops, along with the men from Georgia and Florida."

"Just wait till those Yankees tangle with us," Sammy said. "We'll have them running lickety-split."

"Sammy, do you wish to be excused?" Papa asked quietly.

Captain Trimble continued. "The Confederate Congress has been investigating our military hospitals. Doc, they're a real mess. Fevers, lice, and—"

"I understand," Papa put in quickly. "Go on."

"Well then. Ever since Manassas, the hospitals have been overcrowded. The men . . ." His voice died away and he glanced at me. "This ain't fit for a girl to hear."

"Susanna?" Papa queried.

"I want to stay."

"It's a sight to make a grown man cry," the captain continued. "They lie there burning with fever and all twisted up with pain. There's hardly any medicine."

"I've heard there's not even quinine," Papa said, "except what the blockade runners smuggle in."

"It's the truth. The doctors can't get chloroform, neither. They're taking off arms and legs without anything stronger than a sip of whiskey to dull the pain."

A look that was part pain, part anger flickered on Papa's face. "That's barbaric! I can't believe the Yankee people are so cruel they won't even let medical supplies through."

Sammy set his empty glass on the table. "*I* can believe

it. I heard that when Yankees get really old, their children kill them and eat them."

Neddie snickered. I almost laughed, too, till I saw Papa's scowl. "You're excused, Samuel," he said.

"Yes sir." Leaving his napkin on his chair, he plodded up the stairs. Poor Sammy. He could get into more mischief in one day than Neddie or I could manage in an entire month.

"Forgive me, Captain," Papa said. "Please go on."

"General Lee wants to know if you'll meet him in Charleston the day after tomorrow to plan an inspection of the hospitals. To see if you have any ideas on how to straighten this mess out."

Neddie and I exchanged hasty glances across the table. Surely with a war on, Papa wouldn't leave us. Even if General Lee wanted him. For a moment the only sounds were the ticking of the mantel clock and the whispering of the sea in the tidal creek.

Papa stroked his beard. "When I think of all those young boys lying wounded, some not much older than Neddie, how can I refuse?"

"Then you'll come?" Captain Trimble looked relieved.

"Yes," Papa said. "I will."

It was hard to believe Papa would make such an important decision without consulting us, but there it was.

Papa said, "Allow me to speak to my overseer first and arrange for the care of my children. Tell the general I'll meet him in the city."

"I'll tell him." The captain turned to me. "Appreciate the meal, miss. You'll make a fine plantation mistress someday."

"Oh no." My words tumbled out. "I'm going to be a doctor."

"Is that so? I don't reckon I ever heard of a female doctor."

"Where have you been?" Papa asked. "Elizabeth Blackwell got her medical degree back in 'forty-nine." He put his arm around my shoulder. "Susanna's made rounds with me since she was nine years old. She'll make a fine doctor someday."

Papa's words gladdened my heart. Riding on rounds with him, learning how to mix medicines and heal the sick, was the one thing that made his efforts to turn me into a lady bearable.

"If you say so," the captain said. "But all that book learning is wasted on a girl." He laughed, a most disagreeable sound. "You're young yet. You'll change your mind when some young gentleman takes a fancy to you."

"No, I won't."

"Once Susanna sets her mind to something, she's like a dog on a bone," Papa said. "Come, Captain, I'll see you out."

They went out onto the porch, still talking, their voices low. Neddie sat down on the bottom stair and rested his chin in his hands. "Will Papa send the overseer's wife to stay with us?"

"I don't see how, Neddie. She has four children of her own to look after."

"Maybe Mrs. Miles then."

"Maybe."

"That wouldn't be so bad. Sammy would be happy. He'd have Stephen for a playmate."

"But then it would be lonely for you." I sat on the stair beside him. "Don't you ever wish for a best friend?"

"Don't need one," Neddie said. "I've got you."

I wanted to hug him, but lately he'd acted embarrassed by even the smallest show of affection. So I gave his shoulder a good wallop instead.

He stood up. "Looks like Papa and that captain are going to talk all night. Might as well fetch Sammy and go fishing."

The boys left, and after a while Papa summoned me to the porch.

The tide was out. The damp, fishy breath of the mud-flats hung in the air.

Papa settled into his rocking chair and lit his pipe. I leaned against the porch railing. "Is that horrid man gone?"

"He is." Gray smoke curled over his head. "I don't think he quite knew what to make of you."

"I'm sorry, Papa. I didn't mean to be rude, but I couldn't help it."

"He had it coming," Papa said. "However, for your own sake, my dear, I hope you'll learn to be more tactful. A true lady tempers her speech. She can't always say exactly what's on her mind." He put down his pipe. "Where are the boys?"

"Gone fishing."

"Good. I want to speak with you privately."

Something in his voice made my heart skip. "What is it?"

"There's more to General Lee's request than you know," he began. "It seems there's a fleet of Yankee ships heading this way. Close to fifty in all, Captain Trimble says. Most of them are armed."

"But they wouldn't come to Terrapin Island, would they?"

"They blame South Carolina for starting the war. According to the captain, there are thousands of Yankee soldiers on their way here, too. There's some talk they may try to take Port Royal."

"But that's only forty miles from here!"

His expression was troubled. "That would be the worst possible thing, Susanna. If they capture Port Royal, they could reach Oakwood in two days. Three at the most. We'd be trapped."

"But Papa, what can *you* do about it?"

"The general needs someone who can find out what the Yankees are planning without making them suspicious. By visiting our hospitals, I can travel around, talk to soldiers, listen for information about the Yankees. If I discover anything useful, I'll pass it on to General Lee."

At first it was difficult to fathom his meaning. When at last I did, I could scarcely believe it. Our papa, a Confederate spy.

Chapter Two

The Secret

I STARED AT PAPA in the darkness. The moon came up, painting the tops of the water oaks with a silver light.

"It will be dangerous," he said quietly. "But I have no choice. This war is more than a fight over slavery. Oakwood has been in our family for over a hundred years. I must do whatever I can to protect it."

Perhaps I should have felt proud of Papa, but I was frightened and disappointed that he'd agreed to such a dangerous plan without even talking it over with me. What would become of the boys and me if he were captured or killed?

Extracting an envelope from his pocket, Papa went on. "This is for your cousin Hettie down in Savannah. If anything should happen, if I should be delayed for a long time, find Captain Trimble and give him this letter. He'll see that she comes to take care of you."

The mere thought of Cousin Hettie filled me with dismay. She was so ill-tempered I would rather live with strangers than with her. All the same, I tucked the letter into my pocket.

The boys were returning from the creek. Papa knocked the ashes from his pipe. "I know it's a terrible burden, but you must keep this a secret. The fewer people who know about it, the safer I'll be. Do you understand?"

"Yes, Papa." Hot tears flooded my eyes.

"That's my girl." He stood up and his chair squeaked. "It's only for a short while. Try not to worry."

Sammy and Neddie clattered up the steps. "Look what I brought for you, Papa," Neddie said, holding up his string of fish. "Three bream."

"My favorite!" Papa clapped Neddie on the shoulder. "Thank you, son."

Then Neddie turned to me, his mouth tilted up into a smile. Putting one leg out, he bowed low, like a prince bowing to a queen. "And for you, fair princess, the most beautiful flowers of the field." He handed me a bouquet of cattails, sea oats, and purple asters.

A hard lump settled in my throat. Truth to tell, I was plain as a mud fence. Nobody would ever mistake me for a fair princess. But Neddie was a born gentleman. He could make even a troll feel beautiful.

Sammy tugged at my sleeve. "What's wrong with you?"

"Nothing. I'm perfectly fine."

"Are not," he said. "You're crying 'cause you don't want Papa to go."

"Of course I don't, you little goose."

"I'll bet General Lee makes Papa a general, too," Sammy said. "I'll bet Papa comes back with ten thousand medals and a fine white horse. I'll bet he kills a million Yankees."

"I'm not going to kill anyone," Papa told him. "I'm going to visit the hospitals and then come home. And when I get back, we'll make our Christmas plans."

"Oh, good!" Sammy crowed. "I want a Springfield rifled musket that shoots real ammunition."

"You won't be getting a musket," Papa informed him. "Not this year, anyway."

Sammy stared at Papa as if he couldn't quite believe his ears. "Are you sure?"

"Certain." He lifted Sammy up until their eyes were level. "I'm counting on you to obey Susanna while I'm away. Find some useful way to occupy your time, and do your best to keep out of mischief, all right, Sam?"

Sammy wrapped his arms around Papa's neck. "Yes sir. I know a million ways to keep busy."

Papa chuckled. "That's what worries me."

We went inside. Stopping at his study, Papa said to me, "If you like, you may go with me to the overseer's in the morning. I should check on his daughter's foot before I leave. That was a nasty gash she got last week."

"Yes, Papa." It was his way of making up, but it didn't make me feel the least bit better. Inside my head questions rattled around like marbles in a jar. Who would look after us while Papa was away? Sipsy and Kit? That seemed unlikely. After all, we were accustomed to telling the servants what to do, not the other way around. And suppose something dreadful happened to Papa. What would we do then?

I slept fitfully, waking at the slightest sounds. In the morning, Papa knocked on my door. "Susanna? Wake up."

The floor was cold beneath my feet. I dressed hurriedly and met Papa in the dining room. After breakfast, we went out to our buggy.

Elias was waiting in the shade of the trees. Papa favored him above all our other servants. He was strong and intelligent and could build and fix almost anything. He always carried his tools in a wooden box balanced on his shoulder.

"Elias!" Papa set his medical bag on the porch and shaded his eyes. "What brings you here?"

Elias set his toolbox down. "Mr. Barnes sent me to fix the smokehouse roof. But the fence down by the cow pasture is a-falling down. One good kick and all your cows be a-running six ways to Sunday."

"I see," Papa replied. "This sudden interest in the fence—it wouldn't have anything to do with the fact that it's cooler down by the river than up on the roof, would it?"

"Oh, no sir!" Elias shook his head. "Seem like them cattle be most valuable to you. Seem like you wouldn't want them lost in the woods. Figure on a-fixing that fence and saving you a heap of trouble."

"Did you mention this to Mr. Barnes?" Papa inquired.

Elias stared at his feet. "You know he all full of hisself. A-hollering and a-carrying on like this whole plantation his. He don't like nobody telling him nothing. Figure I best come to you."

Papa said, "I do appreciate it, Elias. But you must follow the overseer's orders. Suppose the hands suddenly began questioning which crops to harvest. Can you see how that could cause trouble?"

Stung by Papa's rebuke, Elias stared past us as if we'd suddenly ceased to exist.

"You go on now," Papa instructed. "Get started on the smokehouse. I'll speak to Barnes about the fence."

Muttering to himself, Elias picked up his tools and walked off. We settled into the buggy. Joseph handed Papa the reins and we curved along the road, past the fields toward the overseer's house.

Papa said, "After you went to bed last night, I rode over to Summerhill to see Mrs. Miles. You and the boys will stay there with her till I come back."

"What about Mr. Miles? Everyone says he's acting strangely these days."

"He seemed all right to me," Papa said. "A bit tired perhaps, but he's not slept well since Darcy left. It must be heartbreaking to see your oldest boy going off to war."

As we drove into the overseer's yard, the chickens squawked and flapped and ran under the porch. Mr. Barnes was in the side yard, chopping firewood. He drove his ax into his chopping block, wiped his hands on his trousers, and came to meet us.

"I apologize for the early hour," Papa said to him. "I have business in the city. Thought we'd check on Lucy's foot before I go."

"Come on in then, if you're a mind to."

We went inside. While Papa removed Lucy's bandage, I opened his medicine bag and took out the salve. But my thoughts returned to poor Mr. Miles. Papa always insists a lady never credits gossip, but everyone on Terrapin Island said Mr. Miles hadn't been himself after Darcy joined the Confederates. People said he'd taken to his bed with his whiskey bottle and lost all interest in his plantation. Even if every word of it were true, there was nothing I could do. Papa had given his word to General Lee.

After Papa put a clean bandage on Lucy's foot, we went outside. Papa said to the overseer, "When will you start the rice harvest?"

"Tomorrow, if there's no rain. Cotton'll be ready this week, too."

"How are the field hands? Sipsy said a few were sick last week."

"You know how they are. Always complaining about something. To hear them talk, you'd think they were never well. Rosie and Peggy both had babies last week. They're useless right now, and here we sit on the biggest cotton crop in years." He swatted at a water bug buzzing around his face. "I can't get blood from a turnip. We need more workers. Plain and simple."

Papa looked thoughtful. "Cotton ought to top sixty cents a pound this year, more for the best quality. Go see

John Thomas over on St. Helena. He owes me a favor. Perhaps he'll rent us some workers."

A frightened look came into the overseer's eyes. "If you ask me, putting a bunch of slaves in a boat is just courting trouble."

"Ask Thomas to send his overseer back with you," Papa advised. "Oh. I almost forgot. Elias came by this morning. Says the fence in the cow pasture is coming down."

"Oh, he did, did he?" Mr. Barnes scratched his arm. "That's one slave that's getting way too big for his britches, to my way of thinking. You'll have trouble with that one before it's all over. Mark my words."

Papa went on as if he hadn't heard. "Take a look at it, will you? And the floodgate in the number eight field is broken, too. Send Elias on over there to fix it."

The overseer's mouth puckered as if he'd just bitten into a green persimmon. "What's the hurry? Won't be no more rice planting till next spring."

"Nevertheless, I'd rather you saw to it now," Papa returned. "Once planting season rolls around again, you'll be too busy. It shouldn't take too long. Elias is handy with tools."

"I've seen better. And I don't aim to put up with him going to you behind my back. You can't expect me to keep these people in line if they know they can run to you for every little thing."

"Do the best you can, Barnes." Papa handed me into the buggy and set his bag inside. "I'll expect a full accounting when I return."

He climbed in, flicked the reins, and we drove out of the yard.

"Why do you keep Mr. Barnes on, Papa? He's always so unpleasant."

"That he is," Papa agreed. "I suppose he's never gotten over losing his own farm. It must sorely try his soul to have to work for me. But with so many men joining the army, I'm lucky to have him. If this war goes on very long, there won't be anyone left to run Oakwood."

We drove on through the cool morning, Papa's little mare stepping smartly along the road. Through the trees, the sun gleamed bright as a gold coin, and the fallen leaves danced in the wind. Usually such an outing with Papa was a happy event, but now that he was going away, sadness pushed the joy from my heart.

Too soon, we were home. Papa's horse was waiting in the shade. Handing the buggy over to Joseph, he picked up his lumpy saddlebags and swung into his saddle.

"No tears, now," he said, smiling down at me. "These are troublesome times, and we all must be brave."

I didn't feel brave. I wanted to jump up beside him, put my arms around him, and hold on for dear life.

"Mrs. Miles will call for you around noon." Papa shifted his weight. The leather creaked. "See that the boys mind their manners, Susanna. And take care of Oakwood. I'm counting on you."

"Yes, Papa. Please be careful, and come back soon."

"I shouldn't be gone more than a couple of weeks. With Mrs. Miles to keep you company, it won't seem like such a long time. Goodbye, my dear. Kiss the boys for me. It's so early, I didn't want to wake them." He turned his horse and was gone.

I went inside. Sammy hurtled along the upstairs hallway, slid down the banister feetfirst, and landed with a thud. "Has Papa left yet?"

"Yes."

"Drat! I wanted to give him my rabbit's foot for good luck."

From his place on the stairs, Neddie winked at me. "You don't really believe in that hocus-pocus, do you, Sammy?"

"The Negroes keep all kinds of things for good luck, even dried-up lizards and snake skins," Sammy said. "I don't reckon a rabbit's foot would hurt. Would it, Susanna?"

"I suppose not. Go upstairs and pack your things now. We're going to stay with Mrs. Miles at Summerhill."

On the porch, we waited for Mrs. Miles's carriage. Twelve o'clock came. Then one o'clock.

"Are you sure she's coming today?" Neddie asked.

"I'm sure." But I worried that she'd forgotten us after all.

Then, up the river road came a lone rider on a gray horse. Sammy jumped up. "That can't be her! Unless we're all going to Summerhill on one old horse."

Neddie squinted into the sun. "I think it's Harrison. Mrs. Miles always makes him wear that black suit."

Harrison rode into the yard. "Miss Susanna? Mrs. Miles say tell you she's powerful sorry, but you can't stay at Summerhill after all."

"What? Why not?"

"Mr. Miles, he feeling most raggedy this morning, and Mrs. Miles say it's more than she can do to take care of the house and Master Stephen and the baby, and all of you, too."

"But she promised Papa!"

"Yessum. She say don't worry none. She a-coming by to visit you next week."

"Next week? What are we supposed to do till then? What if the Yankees—"

Neddie whirled around. "Yankees?"

"It's nothing, Neddie. I was just thinking out loud."

"Well," Harrison said. "I got to go. Mrs. Miles say if I ain't back in one hour, she set the dogs on my trail."

I watched him ride away. I was furious with Mrs. Miles. The prospect of staying at Oakwood alone made me sick with worry. I knew how to clean and dress a wound and how to mix medicines for a fever, but I'd never been in charge of an entire plantation.

Neddie's arm came around my shoulders. "Never mind. We don't need her. We don't need anybody. We can manage just fine. You and me."

Chapter Three

The Plantation

PAPA ALWAYS SAID it was best to be firm with servants, to tell them exactly what you expected. So the next morning I went out to the washhouse where Kit's daughters, Callie and Hannah, were doing the laundry.

The black kettles used for washing clothes were already on the fire in the yard. Baskets of our linens and shirts and my white petticoats were piled up near the doorway. Callie and Hannah were singing.

> *Big ole bull come down the hollow,*
> *Shake his tail, hear him bellow;*
> *Bellow so loud, he jar the river,*
> *Stomp on the earth, make it quiver.*
> *Big ole bull . . .*

Inside the washhouse, it was cool and dim and smelled of soap. Callie and Hannah stopped singing and stared at me.

"Have you washed the bed linens yet?" I asked.

Callie said, "How many years I been doing this family's wash? You think I don't got enough gumption to wash sheets?" She nodded toward the side yard. "They out there, soaking in the kettle, just like always. Nothing change just cause your daddy gone."

"Good. Don't forget to boil Sammy's trousers. And use plenty of soap. They smell like the river."

"*Boil* them?" Callie said. "You can't boil that child's britches! They'll shrink so's a flea couldn't wear them."

"Don't argue with me, Callie. Do as I say."

Callie and Hannah looked at each other. A smile spread across Hannah's face. "You the boss, Miss."

Into the bubbling water went the smelly trousers. Callie tossed in more soap.

"This gonna be enough soap, Miss Susanna?" she asked. "We want to cook up the young master's duds just right."

Hannah's head bobbed like a fishing cork. "Yessum, we surely do! And ain't we the lucky ones, to have you come along to show us just how to do it."

Running Oakwood wasn't as hard as I'd imagined! "Hurry up now. When you finish with the clothes, wash the Sunday tablecloth. And the best napkins. Mrs. Miles is coming next week."

"My my." Hannah put her hand to her back and stretched, like a cat waking up from a nap. "Ain't you something. Acting just like your mama."

"Except Miss Charlotte never made me boil no

britches." Callie speared Sammy's pants with her stick and lifted them up. The hot water streamed back into the kettle.

They were tiny as a doll's clothes.

Ashamed, I grabbed the steaming mess and ran up the path to the house. Sammy and Neddie were playing marbles in the yard.

"What's that?" Sammy asked.

"I'm sorry, Sam." I held them up. "They shrunk."

"What happened?" Neddie picked up his cat's-eye marble and rolled it around on his palm.

"I told Callie to boil them to get the river smell out."

"But I like the river smell!" Sammy said.

"Well, I don't. Not in the house, anyway. Mrs. Miles is coming next week. I want everything to be perfect."

"Mrs. Miles," Neddie snorted. "Don't go to any trouble for her. She probably won't even show up."

"If she does, I want to show her we're doing fine without her."

"Suit yourself," Neddie said. "But if she actually comes out here, I'll eat my hat. Let me see those." He considered the ruined trousers for a moment. "You know what we could do with these? We could make a dummy of a Yankee soldier and hang it in the yard."

Sammy's eyes lit up. "We could put a spear through its heart, like a warning. No Yankees allowed."

Neddie said, "Come on, Susanna. It'll be fun. We can use my old pillow for the body."

The boys were so excited that I soon forgot my mistake. We tied ribbons around the pillow to make a head and body, borrowed one of Papa's shirts, and fashioned a belt from a piece of leather Sammy found in the stable. Then we stuffed the pillow into Sammy's pants and tied the belt around the middle. Because the pillow had no arms, the sleeves of Papa's shirt hung down, but after Neddie drew on a face, it looked exactly like a Yankee, all bug-eyed with sharp, jagged teeth.

"He needs some boots," Sammy decided. "Susanna, you want to boil my shoes?"

Kit came out, carrying her broom, and studied our creation. "What on earth you up to now?"

Sammy held it up. "Look. A Yankee. We're going to put a spear in him. Right through the heart."

"Not before you eat your dinner. I don't aim for it to get cold while you out here messing around. Come on in now and wash up."

We started up the steps. Kit said, "Master Samuel, don't you go messing up Miss Charlotte's parlor. You leave that wet old thing outside, you hear?"

After dinner I went upstairs to write in my journal. Deciding what to record was a pure trial. The washhouse episode made me look foolish, but I couldn't let the servants think they were in charge. Especially not now, when those from other plantations were running away. If I didn't take charge, ours might leave, too. What would happen to Oakwood then?

Despite my mistake, I liked being in charge. Walking through the house, the gardens, and the stables, knowing Oakwood would always be ours, made me feel safe.

At long last, the first week without Papa came to an end. Then the weather turned cool and rainy and we were trapped inside, feeling bored and restless. One day we made paper chains and fastened them over the door to Papa's study. Sammy worked on his Christmas list, and Neddie read to us from his favorite books about Seth Jones and the wild frontier.

Then one morning Mrs. Barnes clattered into the yard in her wagon.

"Whoa!" She pulled on the reins. The horse snorted and tossed its head. "Susanna. I thought you were staying at Summerhill."

"Mr. Miles is sick, so we didn't go there after all."

"Oh. I told your daddy you'd be perfectly safe here with Kit and Sipsy." She lowered her voice. "But he seemed to think you'd be better off with Mrs. Miles. I'm sorry I couldn't come up here myself, but you know how it is with four children around."

She handed me an envelope. "I came by to leave these bills and receipts. Since you're here, you might as well write them in your daddy's account books right away, before they get mixed up or lost."

"Account books?"

"Two big red ledgers. You'll find them in his office. Well, I must go. Luke is in the rice fields today and Lucy's watching the little ones." Taking up the reins, she added, "You'll be all right. Sipsy's been at Oakwood since before your daddy was born. She'll take care of you."

The account books were on the shelf in Papa's office, next to his medical journals and farming magazines. I opened the ledger, then wished I hadn't. Papa's neat writing filled the pages with so many abbreviations I couldn't fathom where anything went.

Mrs. Barnes had brought bills for nails and horse liniment and sugar and molasses from Mr. Miller's store in Charleston. There were receipts for bills Papa had paid and for the first of the crops Mr. Barnes had sold. One said, "52 ac. cot, sold 40 c. Net proceeds $1,038.61."

Net proceeds were what was left after all the bills were paid. But which of the columns was for expenses and which for profits? The numbers at the bottom of each page were the same, but how had Papa made them come out that way? I wrote things down, then drew lines through them and started over again. Soon the ledgers were full of crossed-out lines and splotched with ink.

While I was puzzling it out, Mrs. Miles arrived. From Papa's window, I saw her carriage coming up the road, with Harrison at the reins. Setting the troublesome ledgers aside, I went out to meet her.

Harrison opened the carriage door, and out stepped Mrs. Miles's nursemaid, Liddy, carrying the new baby.

Then came Stephen, then Mrs. Miles herself, so tightly laced into her brown dress that she looked like an over-stuffed sausage.

"My dear!" She kissed the air next to my ear. "I'm truly sorry I was unable to take you in, but you don't seem any the worse for wear."

When I made no reply, she chattered on. "I meant to come sooner, but everything at home is topsy-turvy these days. And the baby's just getting over a wretched cough. It was all too much. You understand."

"Hey, Stephen!" Sammy dashed down the front steps. "Tide's out. Neddie and I are going fishing. Want to come?"

"May I, Ma?" Stephen asked.

She sighed. "Oh, Stephen. In your best clothes?"

"I'll keep clean."

"Well, stay out of the marshes, and don't go far. We can't stay long."

"Don't worry, Mrs. Miles," Sammy said. "We'll be back before you can say *Jack Spratt*."

"I'll depend on that, Samuel."

As soon as we were inside, the nursemaid took the baby upstairs to show her off to Kit. Mrs. Miles and I sat in the parlor. Sipsy brought the tea tray. When she had gone, Mrs. Miles asked, "Any word from your father since he left?"

"No, but he promised to be back within two weeks. I can hardly wait."

"Well of course you can't! Especially with so many Negro uprisings taking place these days. Surely you've heard about poor Mrs. Witherspoon."

I stirred sugar into my tea, wishing I didn't have to hear any news that would increase my worry.

"She was smothered to death in her bed by her own servants. And after all she did for them! I just don't understand it!" She bit into her tea cake. "Oh! I nearly forgot. I had a letter from Darcy last week. Would you like to see it?"

"May I?" From the very first day he'd visited us at Oakwood, Darcy Miles had been a terrible tease, forever pulling my braids or hiding my favorite fishing pole. All the same, his sudden departure had left an empty place in our lives.

She opened her reticule and handed me the letter. "That boy is the very light of my life, but I may as well face it. Ten years of the best tutors money can buy and he still can't spell *cat*."

Dear Mother and Papa,

I take pen in hand to write you a few lines and to let you know that mostly my helth is good and I hope yours is the same. I had a bad stumick ache last week but drank some blackberry tea and feel some better now. Well, Papa, you would be proud of me. I stood guard last night and managed not to fall asleep.

The wether at presant is very cold here. Mother if you can would you send me some more warm socks and some new boots. The soles of my old ones are thin as paper and I can feel every grain of sand under my feet. The food in camp is teribel. I have gone so long without a good meal that I have nearly forgot how to eat. It seems like I have been gone forever. I am tired of camp life and if I live through this war I plan to come home and spend the rest of my life at Summerhill.

How are the crops this year? Write and let me know about the cotton. From what I hear, the price should be good this year. I heard some folks are having trouble with their Negroes, but I am sure that can't be true of ours. They have been with us forever. Tell them hello from me.

Mother, when you see Susanna Simons, ask her to write me a letter. I don't care if it's just a short one. I feel so bad when the mail comes and there is nothing in it for me.

Your loving son forever,
Darcy Miles

I folded the letter and handed it back. "He seems all right."

"I suppose. But I wish he hadn't been so impetuous. Joining the army was just plain foolish. He should be here continuing his schooling and learning how to run Summerhill. What if something happened to my husband? Who would look after things? It's all so overwhelming, I can't think what to do."

Upstairs, the baby started crying. Mrs. Miles stood up. "Oh dear! I'm afraid we should be going. Would you see if you can find Stephen? And tell Harrison we're ready to leave." Hurrying to the foot of the stairs, she called, "Liddy, bring the baby down here. We're going now."

Outside, the driver was sleeping in the shade of the carriage. "Harrison, have you seen my brothers and Master Stephen?"

Just then, the boys rounded the house, Stephen wet and muddy from head to toe, and Neddie and Sammy looking nearly as bad.

"What happened?" I asked.

"The cows got out," Neddie explained. "They kicked the fence loose and got into the mudflats. We went after them."

Elias had said the fence needed fixing. Why hadn't Mr. Barnes seen to it?

"Where are they now?" I asked.

"We found them, all but one," Sammy said. "We piled some brush in front of the broken place. Neddie said that would fool them into thinking the fence was fixed."

Mrs. Miles came down the steps with Liddy and the baby. Upon seeing Stephen in such a state, she cried, "Merciful heavens! What an unholy mess! As if I'm not already burdened enough!"

"I'm sorry, Mother."

"I should hope so. What do you have to say for yourself?"

Neddie explained again about the cows. "Please don't be mad at Stephen. He was only trying to help."

"Well, Stephen," Mrs. Miles said, "you can't sit inside the carriage. You'll have to ride with Harrison."

The arrangement seemed pleasing enough to Stephen. He tossed his muddy shoes onto the carriage roof and climbed up beside Harrison. Mrs. Miles and Liddy settled themselves inside with the baby. Leaning her head out the window, Mrs. Miles said, "Thank you for a lovely tea, Susanna. If you need anything before your father gets back, you just let me know. And don't forget to write to Darcy. It would mean so much to him."

"I won't."

"Well, goodbye, all!"

The carriage rolled down the drive and out of sight. I turned to the boys. "Mr. Barnes should have had the fence fixed last week. But I still don't see how you managed to get so dirty. Surely the cows weren't that hard to catch."

"They weren't," Neddie said.

"Then what happened?"

"We thought we saw some runaways down in the marshes," Neddie said, his voice low. "After we rounded up the cows, we went down there to investigate."

"Runaways? You mean our own servants?"

"Either ours or the Mileses'. We thought we saw two, hiding in the trees."

"But when we got there, they were gone," Sammy said. "We looked everywhere, but we couldn't find them."

Remembering Mrs. Witherspoon, I shivered. But it wouldn't do any good to alarm the boys. "It was probably just fishermen from Petty's Island. They come over here all the time."

"Maybe." Neddie chewed his lip. "But I think we should keep an eye on everybody till Papa gets home."

"Will Stephen tell Mrs. Miles?"

"Oh!" Sammy suddenly snatched Neddie's straw hat. "Hey, Neddie, you need salt and pepper?"

"What are you talking about? Give me back my hat."

Sammy giggled. "You said if Mrs. Miles showed up, you'd eat it."

"Chomp, chomp," Neddie said.

After supper on the porch, Neddie read to us till bedtime. The boys fell asleep easily enough, but I lay awake that night, listening for footsteps on the stairs, imagining Kit and Sipsy coming to murder us in our beds.

On Thursday the sun came out. Joseph put one of Papa's saddles on my horse and led him into the yard. Hannah was sick and Kit was outside helping Callie with the wash. When she saw me, she called out, "Miss Susanna! Where you going?"

"Not far. Cherokee needs his exercise, and I want to speak to Mr. Barnes about the fence. I should check on the cotton, too. Papa says when the weather's damp, you should spread it out to dry."

"Hmmph. You don't need to worry your head about fences and cotton fields. Mr. Barnes know how to take care of everything. You just acting all high and mighty again." She smiled. "Besides, if you go riding off, who gonna show Callie how to do the wash? She need your advice."

"I surely do!" Callie said. "Miss Susanna, I plumb forget. Do I stir them britches this a-way"—she made a big circle with her arms—"or do I stir them that a-way? I stayed up most all night thinking on it, but I just can't figure it out!"

Kit could scarcely disguise her merriment, though I could see nothing amusing. "You got anything need boiling?" she asked. "Got the water nice and hot. Got soap, too. Yessum, I surely do. Plenty of soap, in case they any river smell hereabouts." She and Callie cackled like two hens.

I fed Cherokee a lump of sugar. He was a beautiful horse, smart and well mannered, a present from Papa on my tenth birthday. Next to Papa and Neddie, he was my dearest friend. He swallowed the sugar and twitched his ears, eager to run. Swinging into Papa's saddle, I found the stirrups and tucked my skirts out of the way.

"Lord save us!" Kit cried. "Where your sidesaddle? And how come your skirts all hiked up like that?"

"I told Joseph I wanted Papa's saddle. Skirts are such a bother. I wish I were a boy. Trousers are so much more practical."

"You put your skirt down. You ain't supposed to ride like a man. If your daddy was here . . ."

"But he isn't here, is he? Besides, it's not your place to tell me what to do."

"Some sweet day, child," Kit said. "Some sweet day."

Such a peculiar thing for her to say! But she was right about one thing: There was nothing I could do about the broken fence or the wet cotton. Weary of being in charge, I wanted to forget about ruined laundry and tangled account books and runaways who murdered people in their beds. I wanted to forget my worries about Papa and the Yankees.

Cherokee cantered along the road beside the tidal creek down to the mouth of the river. Leaving him to graze, I took the path to the place where my canoe rested in the marshes.

Here was my special thinking place. It was a wild place, full of shifting shadows, shy creatures, and buzzing insects. Barefoot, holding up my skirts, I waded into the water. The mud, soft and cool as a Sunday pudding, oozed up between my toes. I bent to watch frogs darting through the shallows. On the bank, an old terrapin lumbered along a rotten log. The sun threw patches of yellow light on the water. Mockingbirds fluttered and scolded in the trees.

Even in such a peaceful place it was impossible not to worry about Papa. Was he safe? Where was the Yankee armada, and the thousands of soldiers he'd told me about? Maybe they were here already, waiting to storm our island.

"It won't be long now," I called to Cherokee, "till Papa comes back."

He lifted his head, blinking as if he, too, were eager for Papa's return. I stepped into my canoe and rode the gentle tide, drifting past the pine and cypress trees and along the banks of the rice fields. In the distance, the field hands bent to their tasks, their work songs keeping time with the swish-swish of their reap hooks as the rice stalks fell. Presently it began to rain. I turned back to where Cherokee waited.

He took his time getting us home, picking his way gingerly along the rain-slick road. When at last we splashed into the yard, Neddie burst through the door and down the steps.

"Where have you been?" he shouted.

"I told you I was going to the fields. I didn't mean to be gone so long, but—"

"Never mind. Listen!" His fingers dug into my arm. "The Yankees have captured Port Royal!"

Chapter Four

The Escape

I STARED AT NEDDIE, Papa's words echoing inside my head. *"We'd be trapped . . . The worst possible thing."*

Neddie tugged my arm. "I've been packing ever since we got Captain Trimble's message. We have to hurry, Susanna. If we miss the last ferry—"

"I know that. Where's Joseph? Why isn't he coming for Cherokee?"

"That's the spooky part," Neddie said. "Right after the message came, Sipsy and Kit, Joseph—everybody—just disappeared. One minute they were here, the next they were gone. I think they've all run away."

"What about Mr. Barnes? Surely he'll help us."

"They're gone, too. Sammy saw them heading for the river in a wagon. I've got our wagon hitched in the barn."

Leaving Cherokee in the yard, we hurried inside. In the parlor, Sammy was piling his things into a blanket. He looked up, his eyes shiny with tears.

"Don't be scared, Sammy." I said. "We'll be all right. I promise."

"What are we going to do?"

"We'll take the ferry to Charleston and go to our house on Meeting Street. Then we'll find Papa."

"How?"

"I don't quite know yet. But we'll figure it out."

Neddie said, "I've got some food to eat on the ferry, and the rest of Papa's medicines, and the cash box."

"Good. We'll need money. How much is there?"

"I don't know. It's locked, and I can't find the key."

"Never mind. What else?"

"Matches. We'll need a fire as soon as we get home. I've got Papa's watch."

"Better get the blankets from the cedar chest," I said. "It's getting cold. I won't be a minute."

I gave Sammy my keys. "Go turn the livestock out and then lock the barn. Lock the smokehouse and the cook-house and the stable. Then come straight back."

Upstairs, I changed into a dry dress but didn't take time to pack others. I had a few things at our house in town. Instead, a small likeness of my mother and the gold-and-garnet bracelet she'd worn the day she married Papa went inside my reticule, along with Papa's letter to Cousin Hettie.

"Susanna! Hurry up! We'll miss the ferry!" Neddie had brought the wagon around. Sammy leaped onto the porch, my keys jingling in his hand. "I locked it all up," he reported. "Just like you said."

We went down the steps. Cherokee was still standing patiently beneath the dripping trees. I removed his saddle and shoved it beneath the porch. He nickered softly and tossed his head, uncertainty showing in his chocolate-colored eyes. Something inside my chest cracked open. I threw my arms around his warm, wet neck, shielding the boys from the sight of my tears.

Sammy and I climbed on the wagon. Neddie patted my arm. "Don't worry about old Cherokee. He's the smartest horse in Carolina. If the Yankees show up, he'll hide in the woods till they've gone. He'll be all right." Then he called to the mule, "Ho, Fanny! Get up!" and we clattered toward the ferry.

I could have made it in no time riding Cherokee, but the wagon was clumsy, and Fanny plodded along as if we were only out for a Sunday ride. I turned around on the seat.

"Don't look back." Neddie's voice was tight. "It'll make you feel worse."

But I couldn't help it. Oakwood grew smaller and smaller, floating in the mist like something in a dream.

Suddenly Elias's son, Benjamin, wild-eyed and trembling, stepped into the road in front of us and grabbed Fanny's neck. "Stop the wagon!"

"Let go before I run over you!" Neddie yelled.

"Miss Susanna? You got to come quick. My daddy hurt."

Neddie yanked on the reins. "We don't have time. Get out of the way."

"Wait, Neddie," I said. "What happened, Benjamin?"

"Why should we care?" Neddie asked. "It serves him right for running off when Papa's not around."

"Please, miss." Benjamin's lips quivered in the cold. "He was a-fixing a gate, and the saw slip. He bleeding bad."

I couldn't think. We had to catch the ferry. Elias was one of our most valuable slaves, but I'd never done any doctoring without Papa to guide me.

"What about your mother?" I asked. "Tell her to wrap the cut very tight till the bleeding stops. Then give him some ginger root tea. He'll be all right."

"She can't. She too scared." He hopped from one foot to the other. "Please. You got to help."

Neddie said to me, "Come on, Susanna. We're running out of time."

"I can't let him bleed to death, Neddie. What would Papa say?"

"Go on, then! Never mind about us! You're just like Papa. Always worrying about everybody else."

"Where's the medicine chest?"

"You're not going down there alone," Neddie said. "I'm coming with you."

Sammy said, "I'm not staying here by myself. What if the Yankees come?"

Bending close to Neddie's ear, I whispered, "You have to stay here to protect the wagon from the runaways. I'll be back soon."

He took out Papa's watch. "Ten minutes and then I'm coming for you."

Benjamin led me along the muddy path to the quarters. In one corner of their cabin was Elias's toolbox, a big cloth bundle, and a lantern with a blackened wick. A kettle bubbled in the grate, filling the cabin with the smell of pork and collard greens.

Elias lay on a straw mattress on the dirt floor, a bloody rag wrapped around his arm. His wife, Ruth, set a basin of water on the floor.

She wouldn't look at me. Instead, her eyes darted from the empty yard to the window and back again. Benjamin watched from the corner.

I washed my hands and unwound the bloody bandage. The cut was deep, but luckily the blood wasn't spurting. "I need some clean cloth, Ruth. That bundle in the corner will be fine."

"That for a baby grave. Died last week. We having the funeral celebration tomorrow." She untied her head kerchief, but it was slick with dirt and sweat and crawling with lice.

"Creation! That won't do! You ought to worry more about Elias than a baby who's already dead!" I took off my petticoat.

"What you doing?"

"Making a clean bandage. Hurry up. Hold this."

With the torn strips of my petticoat, I washed the wound, then shook some powdered alum from Papa's medicine chest into it. I fashioned a tight bandage and tied it off. "There! It's done!"

Taking up the medicine chest, I hurried back along the slippery path to the wagon.

Neddie pulled me onto the seat and shouted to the mule, and we started off again.

Sammy said, "Is Elias dead?"

"No, Sammy. He cut his arm."

"How bad is it?"

"Bad, but he'll be all right."

"It was a waste of time," Neddie said. "They're the last ones here, and they'll be gone as soon as he can stand on his feet."

Nearing the road to Summerhill, we saw Darcy's little mare running in circles under the wet trees. The Mileses' cattle stood in the roadway, bawling.

"They've gone, too," Sammy said.

The minutes ticked away. Finally we reached the ferry crossing, but there was no ferry in sight.

"This is odd. Where's the boat?" Neddie pulled out Papa's watch. "We should have five minutes to spare."

"Where are the Mileses and the Barneses?" I wondered. "They had to have come this way."

"I bet they took the one that comes at noon," Sammy said. "I wish we'd been on it, too. I wish we were already in Charleston."

"Wait here," Neddie said. "I'll go ask what's happened."

In a moment he was back.

"The ferry's not coming," he reported. "Service is suspended till further notice. There's a note on the door."

"Suspended?" Sammy asked. "What does that mean?"

"It means we have to find another way to get off the island," I said.

"How?" Sammy demanded.

"I don't know!" I cried. "Stop bothering me! I don't know the answer to everything!"

"I've got an idea," Neddie said after a time.

"The flatboat?"

"Yes. There's still rice in the fields. One of our boats must be empty."

"I thought of that, too, Neddie, but that boat's too big for the three of us."

"What about your canoe?" Sammy asked. "I can paddle it just fine."

"Too small," Neddie and I said together.

"The flatboat's the only way," Neddie said. "We can't just sit here and wait for the Yankees to show up. They'll probably be here by this time tomorrow."

"But the flatboat's a long way from here."

"Four or five miles at least," he agreed.

"We can't make it before dark."

"Not in this contraption," he said. "Especially if we take the road all the way back around."

"We'll have to leave the wagon here and walk."

"Jehoshaphat!" Sammy exclaimed. "We can't walk that far. We should take Fanny."

Neddie turned around on the wagon seat. "All three of us? On that poor old heap of buzzard bait?"

"We could take turns riding. I'll go first."

"I'll just bet you would!" Neddie said. "You always think of yourself before anybody else."

"That's not true!" Sammy balled his fists. "I guess you have a better idea, Mr. Brilliant-with-Your-Nose-in-a-Book."

"Yes I do," Neddie said. "Susanna's in charge. We'll let her decide."

Taking the mule with us would be too dangerous. If we chanced upon Yankee soldiers, it would be harder to hide with Fanny along. And it was growing late. Even if we rode, we couldn't reach the flatboat before nightfall.

"We'll spend the night here. In the wagon," I decided. "And tomorrow we'll turn Fanny loose and walk to the flatboat."

"What about the soldiers?" Sammy asked. "What if they shoot at us here in the dark?"

"They couldn't have made it all the way from Port Royal yet," Neddie said. "But we'll take turns keeping watch, just in case. Just like real Confederate soldiers. What do you say, Sammy? You and I can take the first watch while Susanna sleeps."

"All right," Sammy said. "But I sure wish I had a Springfield musket."

"We'll be fine," Neddie said. "If the soldiers come, we'll hide in the trees. We know these woods better than they do. They could never find us in a million years."

We unhitched the wagon and led the mule down to the water.

"I'm hungry!" Sammy said. "I'm so hungry I could eat soap."

We ate the biscuits and some of the meat Neddie had brought. Soon night came down. Huddled beneath our blankets in the wagon, we listened to the owls and whip-poorwills and the night creatures rustling in the thicket.

Neddie moved beneath the blanket. "Should we really stand watch?"

"I don't know."

We'd spent so much time in the woods that I should have felt at home there. On warm evenings, we'd chase fireflies or play hide-and-seek or fish by lantern light. But if I ever felt afraid, I had only to look back toward the house to see yellow lamplight shining through the trees, or the red glow of Papa's pipe as he sat on the porch, watching over us. Now there was no welcoming light, no one to keep us safe. Tomorrow we'd be on our own, on the flatboat.

Flatboats were not fast and graceful, like sailing yachts, or powerful, like steamers. They were simple wooden boats thirty feet long and ten feet wide, with flat bottoms. There was an oar for steering and long poles to propel them along the river. Even at high tide, they were heavy and hard to steer. At low tide they were likely to stick in the mud or snag on the dead branches lying below the surface. If we missed the morning tide, we would have to wait till evening. And while we waited, the Yankees would be coming ever closer.

All night I dreamed of being chased by Yankee soldiers. When I woke up, the birds were fussing in the trees and the sky was full of light. The boys were still sleeping, leaning toward each other like two uprooted trees. I shook them awake.

"Come on. Sun will be up soon."

When we had eaten, Neddie trimmed a stick, threaded it through the knot in our food bundle, and hoisted it onto his shoulder. I carried Papa's medicines and my reticule, and Sammy shouldered his bundle.

I slapped Fanny's rump. The mule plodded into the trees, and we started walking.

Chapter Five

The River

WE FOLLOWED THE RIVER through stands of water oaks and feathery cypress trees, through sea grasses, and shallow creeks that ran out to the sea. For some time we walked without speaking until Sammy stopped and said, "Hold it!"

"What now?" Neddie muttered.

"I'm hungry."

"We're all hungry, Sammy, but we have to keep going," I said.

"But I'm about to perish." He had that mutinous look in his eye that meant trouble.

"Five minutes," I said. "Then we'll have to walk even faster to make up for it."

Beneath the sheltering trees, we ate some dried peaches and the rest of the meat. I tucked the last of the food back into the blanket. "We'll save what's left until we're safely across the river."

"We'll never get there at this rate." Neddie tossed a twig into the water and it swirled away. He had taken it upon himself to get us safely off the island, too much responsibility for a boy of eleven.

"Don't worry, Neddie. It can't be too much farther. Ready, Sam?"

We set off again, Neddie in the lead. Sammy trudged along with his head down, a pinched look on his face. It pained me to see him looking so scared.

"Sammy," I said, "it's only seven weeks till Christmas. Have you finished your list yet?"

"Mostly." His mouth curved into a smile.

"Tell me."

We were walking fast and his words came out in spurts. "If I don't get . . . the musket . . . then I want . . . a chess set and . . . a harmonica . . . and—"

"Hey!" Neddie turned, waving his arms. "There's a boat."

Usually the path from the rice fields to the boat landing was crowded with our field-workers loading the harvest for the journey downstream. But today it was deserted. An empty flatboat rode high on the morning tide, turning slowly on its tether.

Neddie grinned. "We'll be across this old river before you know it."

Hurrying aboard, we stowed our bundle and found the oar and the poles. The boat creaked and steadied on the water.

"You steer," I said to Neddie. "We'll push."

Neddie moved to the back of the boat, and Sammy and I took our places on either side. "Push!" I shouted, and we slid away from the shore.

At first it was almost possible to forget about the Yankee soldiers and our runaways. A soft breeze made little ripples on the shining water. On the gentle current, we glided past our fields, past rows of shadowy green trees bordering the river.

But that was before my hands grew red and blistered and my arms began to ache, quivering beneath the weight of the pole. Neddie, his brow shiny with sweat, fought to keep the boat near the middle of the river.

"Let's change places, Neddie." Pulling my pole from the water, I took over the oar. Neddie slid the pole back into the water and pushed.

The longest part of our journey lay ahead. Soon the river would widen into rougher water, and then, as the tide went out, steering would become even more difficult. There was no hope of reaching the city before nightfall. We would have to spend the night on the river.

"Log!" Neddie cried.

Too late. Summoning all my strength, I pulled desperately on the oar, but the boat was too heavy. We hit the log broadside and spun around and around in the current, the boat shuddering and dipping, sending brown water swirling over our feet. Neddie fell hard as the boat bucked and spun toward a clump of logs and dead leaves.

"Are you all right?" I yelled.

"Just pull!"

The water poured over the side again, sending Sammy facedown onto the bottom of the boat. "Susanna! My pole!"

We watched helplessly as it drifted out of reach.

"Help me!" I shouted.

Sammy took the oar. Neddie pushed our only pole deep into the water, straining against the river until the boat steadied at last.

"That was close!" he said.

"It was all my fault," I said. "And now we've lost a pole."

"I didn't mean to!" Sammy cried. "I tried to hold on, but I couldn't. I *told* you we should have taken the canoe!"

"There's nothing we can do now," I said. "We'll just have to make do."

"If only we could rest awhile," Neddie said. "I'm so tired I could sleep for a week."

But we kept going.

By late afternoon, we had reached the top of the wide **S** curve of the river, a place so narrow that I could almost touch either bank with my pole. Although it was still light, we stopped for the night.

Giddy with relief, Neddie stowed the pole and grinned. "Who's hungry?"

I dropped onto the bank, as weak as water. "I am."

"How about you, Sammy? Hungry?"

"Not for more dried-out meat. I'd rather eat horse-shoes."

Taking a line and a hook from his pocket, Neddie said, "Let's have fish tonight."

"Are we cooking it?" Sammy asked. "I'm not eating it raw."

"We'll build a fire and roast the fish over the coals. Just like Seth Jones on the frontier." He trapped a water bug and baited his hook. "I hope the fish are biting."

A few minutes later, Neddie cried, "Got one!" and jerked on his line. A silvery fish flopped into the boat.

Sammy looked happier than he had since we'd left Oakwood. "I'll make the fire by myself."

He cleared a place near the shore and gathered twigs and moss. We lit a match and Sammy blew on the smoldering twigs till the flame caught. By the time the fire had burned down to hot coals, Neddie had prepared three fish. We roasted them on sharpened sticks and pulled the meat off with our fingers. For dessert we ate some berries I'd picked.

When darkness came, I said, "You sleep first, Neddie."

"I'll stay awake," Sammy said. "I'll protect you with my knife."

"Come on, then." Using one of our blankets, I fashioned a pillow and we settled in. Neddie curled beneath a blanket, and his breathing grew deep and even.

The boat rocked like an enormous cradle. Sammy yawned, and his eyelids drooped. Soon, he was fast asleep.

Night on the river was beautiful and mysterious. I watched the stars glittering like candles in the dark, and the ripple of silver moonlight on the water, listening to the songs of the night creatures, until I too, fell asleep.

The smell of smoke woke me.

The boys were still asleep. The sky glowed pink through the curtain of mist rising off the water. A bright flame danced where our supper fire had been.

I stepped off the boat. A quiet voice whispered, "Miss Susanna?"

"Who's there?"

Elias appeared out of the shadows, wearing an old hat low over his eyes, and a coat that brushed the tops of his shoes. Tucked under his good arm was the bundle I'd seen in his cabin.

"What are you doing here?" I demanded. "Why aren't you back at Oakwood where you belong?"

"Nobody at Oakwood now. The Yankees a-coming, and we all free."

What a goose I'd been, risking our safety to tend him, when all along he was betraying us. "So you're leaving, too. Just like the rest of them. That cloth wasn't for a grave. It was for running away! How could you?"

"Freedom so important, a body will do anything to get it. But I don't expect you can understand how it . . ."

"Oh, I understand perfectly. You waited till Papa left and then you deserted us, just when he counted on you to look after Oakwood. But you don't care about it at all!"

He shrugged. "Ever since my baby-time I been a-building things for your pappy. Done made Oakwood into the finest plantation hereabouts. But not one stick of it belong to me."

"And you came all this way to tell me you're running off?"

"Susanna?" Neddie sat up. "What is it?"

"It's Elias."

Neddie jumped off the boat. "What are you doing here? You get back to work right now, or I'll make you wish you had!"

Elias's expression went hard as stone. "Ain't never going back there."

"You have to," Neddie said. "If you don't, it's the same as stealing."

Sammy followed Neddie off the boat. He said to Elias, "I hope they catch you. I hope they throw you in jail and make you live on beans and water for the rest of your life."

Elias seemed not to hear. He said to me, "I been following the river, same as you. Saw you hit that log in the water. This old boat too much for you to handle."

"We've managed so far."

"Yes'm, I reckon so. But a storm a-coming." He pointed to dark clouds gathering in the sky. "Once it hit, you gonna be tossed around like a matchstick in a hurricane."

"We'll wait it out," Neddie said. "We'll turn the boat over and use it for shelter till the storm passes."

"You can't turn over a boat that big," Elias said. "Face up to it. You in as much trouble as I am."

Turning to me, Elias said, "When I cut my arm, you coulda passed right on by. But you didn't, so I got to pay you back."

"Pay me back? Haven't we always taken care of you?"

"Yes'm, but I ain't a slave no more. And I got my pride." He cocked his head. "I can take the boat down the river, till you safe on the other side."

Neddie said, "What about bounty hunters? There's a reward for runaways."

"Don't nobody but you know I'm running," Elias said. "Anybody stop us, you just say, 'Why, Mr. Bounty Hunter, suh, this here be our old slave Elias, faithful as a shadow, taking the massa's chillen to safety.'"

He looked up and down the riverbank, then back toward the flatboat. Something other than pride had brought him here. "You want our boat!" I said. "That's why you followed us!"

"Some folks a-waiting for me on downriver, and yes'm, I can get there a heap faster in this boat than a-walking."

"A heap safer, too," Neddie said. "You ought to be ashamed, hiding behind us."

"Nothing more shameful than being a slave," Elias declared. "But you right. Pattyrollers won't stop me long as I'm with you."

Thunder rolled in the distance. "Seem like we need each other, Miss Susanna." I didn't want his help. If I accepted it, I was aiding his escape. But we were tired, nearly out of food, and a storm was rolling in.

Elias shifted his bundle. "Make up your mind. 'Cause one way or the other, I got to be moving on."

"Neddie?"

He shrugged. His eyes looked so hollow and frightened, my heart nearly broke.

"All right. But don't think Papa won't come looking for you when he gets back."

Another roll of thunder hastened our steps. Elias smothered the fire and handed me a long branch. "For that pole you lost."

We left on the morning tide. With Elias, the trip went much faster. The shore sped past as we traveled downriver. Soon we passed the end of Papa's property, and the Summerhill boat landing.

Then the storm hit, bringing a curtain of windswept rain. Planting his feet at the back of the boat, Elias manned the oar. The boys and I shared the poles. The wind whipped the river into icy whitecaps that splashed over the sides of the boat, numbing our fingers and toes. Lightning crackled and arced across the angry sky.

"Left!" Elias shouted. "Left! Watch now. She gonna dip here!"

The boat shuddered, pitching and rising on the water.

"Susanna!" Sammy yelled. "I'm scared!"

"Don't let go, Sammy! Hold on!"

Elias's bundle came open. Something hard and shiny rolled against my feet. My mother's silver sugar bowl.

I remembered Elias telling Papa about the broken fence, pretending to be so concerned about the cattle. All the time he was planning to steal from us.

"Miss Susanna!" Elias yelled. "You got to pull! Pull, or she gonna roll!"

An enormous wall of water rolled toward us. Tightening my grip, I leaned into the wind and fought the current.

"All right now. Bring her right! Hold her steady." Elias's gaze swept over the silver bowl at my feet. "Here come the next wave!" he shouted. "Pull now!"

Hours seemed to pass. Eventually the wind died and the city appeared on the horizon.

Elias guided the boat into a shallow cove. While the boys uncoiled the line, I gathered our soggy blankets and the silver bowl. The boat bumped against the pilings and Neddie jumped ashore and made fast the line.

Tossing aside the oar, Elias said, "Reckon now you plan on sending the slave catcher after me. 'Specially on account of that bowl."

"It's ours," Neddie said. "You had no right to take it."

"So the law people say. But that bowl a mighty small payment for a whole lifetime a-working on your pappy's plantation."

I hesitated, then handed him the bowl.

"What are you doing?" Neddie cried. "Don't give him that!"

For a moment Elias stood there. Then he hid the bowl inside his bundle. Turning his collar up against the wind, he said, "Well, Miss Susanna, I reckon we about as even as we can be."

And without looking back, he disappeared into the swirling mist.

Chapter Six

The City

LEAVING THE FLATBOAT heaving and bumping in the cove, we set off for our house, climbing the hill near the old shipyard and on past the warehouses and loading docks till we reached the battery.

"There they are," Neddie said quietly. Through the mist, Yankee gunboats appeared, scattered along the horizon.

We turned up cobblestone streets slick with rain. Ahead of us the church steeples pointed like long white fingers to the sky. The houses along Tradd Street were dark and shuttered behind their iron gates. In the gardens, the last of the autumn flowers drooped in the rain. It seemed we were the only people in all of Charleston, all was so quiet.

But Queen Street was a tangle of wagons and carriages and carts piled high with baggage. Farmers in rough clothes and scuffed boots jostled gentlemen shouting orders to their servants. Ladies scurried through the rain, their shiny black umbrellas sprouting like mushrooms in a forest.

"Where's everybody going?" Sammy asked.

"I don't know." There was so much bustle and commotion, so many people hurrying through the streets, it was hard to know who was coming and who was going.

It was dark when we reached our house, too late to begin my search for Papa. Although we'd left the house only weeks before, a carpet of gray dust had settled on the floors. Cobwebs swayed in the sudden gust of wind coming through the open door. The chairs and tables, covered with blankets to keep off the dust in our absence, filled the parlor with lumpy shapes and deep shadows.

"This is spooky," Sammy said, "and I'm frozen half to death." He blew on his fingers to warm them. "I wish Sipsy and Kit were here."

"We'll make a fire and thaw out, all right, Sam?"

"I'm hungry, too," he said. "When can we eat?"

"Hold your horses," Neddie said. "First things first."

While Neddie looked for the lamps, I hurried to set the house to rights. When he lit a match and turned up the wick, the yellow light made the house seem more cheerful. The boys searched the cupboards for food, and I went upstairs to prepare our beds. The smells of lavender and camphor drifted up from the cedar chest where the linens were stored, a comforting thing at the end of such a difficult journey. When the beds were made, I went down to the kitchen.

"Look!" Sammy crowed, holding up a jar. "Real strawberry jam."

"Anything to go with it?" I asked.

"Some dried turnips," Neddie said. "Three carrots. And some onions. I guess we could make soup."

While Sammy pumped water, Neddie lit a fire in the grate. I filled one of the cooking pots with water, guessing at the amount, added the wrinkled-up vegetables, and set the pot in the hearth. It wouldn't be much of a supper. Despite all my book learning, I knew little that was useful in real life.

We ate in front of the fire. There were too many onions and not enough carrots, and the turnips had cooked to a bitter mush, but the boys didn't complain. For dessert, we ate the last of the dried peaches we'd brought from Oakwood and jam right from the jar.

Sammy smiled a red-ringed smile. "Susanna, when we get back to Oakwood, you can do all the cooking."

I wanted to weep. The soup pot was empty, and we were still hungry. I wished for a platter of Sipsy's fried chicken, the outside browned to a turn, the inside hot and juicy, and one of her Sunday cakes with boiled icing.

Sammy's spoon clanked into the empty jam jar. "I'm so tired I could sleep for a hundred years."

"Me too," Neddie said. "I'm so sore my hair hurts."

We banked the fire and went upstairs.

A while later, Neddie knocked once and opened my door. "Susanna? You awake?"

He came in, carrying Papa's cash box. "I got this thing open, but there's not nearly as much money as I expected."

"How much?"

"Only about eleven dollars. And a bunch of IOUs from people Papa doctored last summer."

"Don't worry about it. Tomorrow I'll speak to the general and he'll send Papa straight home."

"What if the general's not here?" Neddie asked.

So distressing was that prospect that for a moment the burden of Papa's secret was almost too much to bear. But I was sworn to silence. "Surely someone at headquarters will know where the general is. And the general will know where Papa is."

"You're right," Neddie said. "There are only so many hospitals for Papa to visit. He's bound to be on his way back by now."

I burrowed beneath my covers. Neddie said, "I'm sorry I got mad at you the other day. You were right to help Elias when he was hurt. Even if he did turn out to be a traitor and a thief."

"Oh, Neddie, you didn't mean it. You were scared."

"He's hard to understand. I wonder what he'll do with Mama's bowl."

"Sell it. Or trade it for something he needs for Ruth and Benjamin."

"Where were they when he was on the river?"

"Heading north, I suppose, or hiding with the abolitionists. There are people all over helping runaways escape."

"Abolitionists! They're no better than thieves! They should all be put in jail." He was quiet for a moment. "I wonder whether he'll make it. And Kit and Sipsy, too. I never figured on their turning against us."

"Until Papa posts a reward notice, nobody will be looking for any of them."

"If he comes home tomorrow, we can put up a notice at the newspaper office," Neddie said. "Maybe we can still get Elias back. Even if we can't go back to Oakwood, there's plenty of work that needs doing right here." He set the cash box on the table beside my bed. "Sweet dreams."

We woke to the clatter of horses' hooves on the cobblestones and the songs of street vendors. Sammy burst into my room, his hair sticking out, his cheeks still pink from sleep.

"I'm hungry!" he announced as if this were highly unusual.

"You know there's no food yet. You'll have to wait."

He sat cross-legged on the floor, watching while I washed my face and braided my hair. Then he picked up my reticule and sniffed it. "Too bad the servants have run off. This thing smells awful. It needs boiling."

"Put that down!"

"Are you going to Mr. Miller's store?" he asked.

"Of course."

"Will you stop at the confectionery and get some lemon drops? I haven't had any in a crow's age!"

"No lemon drops. We've only a few dollars to last till Papa gets back."

"Not even *one*? One wouldn't cost much, Susanna."

"Not even one. But if you're good, when Papa gets here, I'll ask him to buy a whole bag. How's that?"

He crossed his arms over his chest. "A whole bag to *share*, or a whole bag each?"

"A whole bag each, all right, Sam? Now go wash up. And comb your hair. You look a fright."

I woke Neddie, took the money from the cash box, and stepped out onto the street.

The bell above Mr. Miller's door jingled when I went in. Mr. Miller was behind the counter reading the newspaper. "Susanna Simons! Thank goodness you made it back to town. They say the Yankees are turning the Sea Islands into a regular no-man's-land. Makes me so mad, I wish I was young enough to join the army myself. Well, what can I do for you?"

Behind him were shelves of sugar and salt, jars of jam, tins of spices and dried meats. Flour and potatoes, onions and turnips sat in barrels on the floor, adding to my bewilderment. All my life Sipsy and Kit had been in charge of our kitchen. I'd been there only a few times with my mother when she wanted to serve something special. But I didn't want to look foolish in front of Mr. Miller. I chose potatoes and onions and jam, some tins of cinnamon, and something called sage, and opened my reticule. "That will be all today."

He frowned. His bushy white brows and round little eyes made him look like the herons that lived on our island. "Who all came back from the island with you? Where's your cook?"

"The servants have all run off," I said. "And Papa is away. It's just my brothers and me."

"All by yourselves in that big old house?"

"I can manage."

"Yes, I expect you can at that. But you'll need flour and salt, Susanna. And some lard for making bread."

"I haven't much money just now."

"Don't worry about it. I'll put it on your bill." He scooped flour into a muslin bag and tied it tight with twine. "On second thought, no I won't. Consider it a favor."

"Sir?"

"Your daddy took care of my oldest boy when he came home from Manassas with his leg missing. It nearly destroyed his poor mother to see Clay looking like that, but I suppose we should be grateful he came back at all. So many didn't."

Then I remembered the sad day back in July when the dead were brought home from the battlefield. There had been a special ceremony at the train station. Papa and I stood there together in the dizzying heat, watching our wounded soldiers parade past with the coffins. Later, one of Papa's friends scolded him for allowing me to witness such a dreadful scene. He said it wasn't a proper thing for a young girl to see, but the war had erased all the polite rules we had once lived by. When autumn came we had returned to Oakwood, and the memory faded until it seemed like something I'd only read about in a book.

Now, Mr. Miller said, "Your daddy wouldn't accept a penny for taking care of Clay. Said it was the least he could do for the Confederacy. The least I can do is put food on your table while he's away."

I put everything into a string bag I'd found in the cupboard. "Thank you, Mr. Miller."

"Not at all, my dear. You be careful now. The streets are filling up. Some folks have gone plumb crazy trying to get out of town before the Yankees get here."

"The Yankees? Coming here?"

"Don't you worry," Mr. Miller said. "It's nothing but rumors. The Yankees won't even get close. You'll see."

When I got home, Neddie yanked open the door. "What took you so long? Sammy won't do a thing I say."

"I'm sorry, Neddie. It was so hard to know what to choose, and I haven't the faintest notion how to cook."

"I'll help." Sammy stood behind Neddie, his hair still sticking out like straw in a bird's nest. "I can peel vegetables." He held up his little pocket knife. "It's sharper than it looks." Then he peered into my bag. "Oh, good! Potatoes! We can make hash browns, and biscuits and gravy and jam."

"If only I knew how."

Neddie said, "I was poking around in the pantry and look what I found." He pulled out a dog-eared receipt book.

"Thank goodness! Neddie, what would I do without you?"

"I have no idea." He grinned. "I'm indispensable."

"Come on, let's see if we can figure out these receipts."

We went out to the kitchen. While Neddie lit the fire, I read the directions for making biscuits and rolled the dough with Sipsy's rolling pin. Sammy insisted on peeling the potatoes with his knife. While the biscuits cooked, I set a skillet on the fire and melted some lard. Then I sliced the potatoes, mixed them with flour and salt, and dropped them into the hot grease.

"We need a lid."

Neddie found one and set it over the pan.

"I need butter," Sammy said. "And milk. I'm thirsty."

"Well, we won't have any today. After breakfast, I'm going to army headquarters to ask about Papa. When he comes home, we'll have milk, all right?"

The biscuits turned out black as coal and hard as stone.

"Maybe the insides are still soft," Neddie said hopefully. He tried to slice one, but it slid off his plate and thudded onto the floor like a lump of lead.

"Susanna, don't throw them out," Sammy said. "Maybe the army can use them for ammunition."

"Hush your mouth, Sammy," Neddie said. "Unless you can do better."

I lifted the lid on the skillet. The potatoes floated like brown lily pads in their pond of hot lard. Sammy speared one out, blew on it to cool it, and popped it into his mouth. "Susanna, these are really good!"

After we'd eaten our fill of hot potatoes and jam, we washed the plates and put away the skillet and the rolling pin. When everything was in order, I said, "I'm going to find Papa. While I'm gone, Neddie is in charge."

"Oh, drat!" Sammy grumbled. "Neddie is always in charge."

"That's because he's older than you. But you can be second in command. All right?"

"Second in command?" His little face lit up. "What does that mean?"

"Well," Neddie said. "If I fall down stone dead, you get to be in charge."

"You mustn't tease about such things, Neddie," I said. "I'll be back as soon as I can. If you need anything, go see if Mrs. Miles is home yet. You know her house. The big white one on Friend Street."

"Yes. Go on now. The sooner Papa gets here, the better."

The streets were full of people scurrying in and out of doorways. Carriages clattered along the streets. On the corner, a drayman's wagon blocked my way. Two men came down the steps of a red brick house carrying trunks, hat boxes, and wooden crates. Despite Mr. Miller's assurances, it seemed everyone was leaving.

With so many people coming and going even the air seemed troubled. What was happening? Was there even time to ask after Papa?

A man carrying a silver-handled cane hurried past.

"Pardon me, sir. What . . ."

"Sorry, miss. I'm late for my train." And he pushed past me so quickly that my ankle cracked against the cobblestones.

On I went, searching for a friendly face, but everyone seemed too worried and too busy to notice me. At last I stopped a street vendor heading for the market. "Pardon me!"

She opened her basket. "Vegetables, miss?"

"No, thank you. I'm looking for the Confederate headquarters and I'm in an awful hurry. Do you know where it is?"

"Headquarters?"

"The army!" I cried. "General's Lee's office."

"Oh. Across the street and down that alley. There's a sign on the door."

A sentry at the door touched the brim of his hat as I came up the steps. Inside, a dark-haired soldier sat writing at a desk. Without looking up, he held up one hand, signaling me to wait. With every tick of the clock, my uneasiness grew. Suppose the soldier didn't believe me? Suppose he refused to help me find Papa? I hid my shaking hands inside my skirts and swallowed the papery feeling in my throat.

Finished at last, he turned to me, his expression a mixture of amusement and surprise.

"I'm afraid you've made a mistake," he said, smiling. "The hat shop is two doors down."

"I'm not shopping for hats. Is Captain Trimble here? It's very important."

"He's out on a special detail. I'm Captain Griffith. What can I do for you?"

"I'm Susanna Simons. I came to see General Lee."

"Did you now? And what would you be wanting with the general?"

"He asked my father to visit the hospitals for him. We had to leave Terrapin Island because the Yankees came."

To my utter horror, my voice cracked when next I spoke. "We . . . we're alone now and we want Papa back. My little brothers and I."

"You came here all alone?"

"Yes. Our servants have all gone, too. I *must* find him."

He set his papers aside. "When the Federals attacked Port Royal, General Lee moved closer to the front."

"Where did he go? Is my father with him?"

He motioned to a chair. "Please, dear. Sit down."

I sat. The captain said, "I'm sorry, but I can't tell you where your father is."

His eyes were so full of kind feeling for me that I feared I would weep. Taking up his pen he said, "I could try sending a message to him, if you'd like."

"Oh yes! Please." Relief made my words tumble out too fast. "He's Dr. William Simons. Tell him we're here, but we need him to come home now. Before the Yankees capture Charleston."

"I'll tell him, but you needn't worry about that. You're safe here."

"If it's so safe, why is everyone leaving?"

"Some folks have panicked, but there's no cause for concern."

"You promise you'll send Papa a message? Right away?"

"Upon my word as an officer and a gentleman."

"When will he receive it? How soon will he be home?"

"Slow down a minute. That all depends on whether we can find him in the first place, and how far away he is."

"But what is your best guess?" I asked. "Could he be here by tonight? Tomorrow?"

"Impossible to say. He could be anywhere. Georgia maybe. Or down in Florida."

"Surely you know where *General Lee* is. Find him, and he'll know where my father is."

"Yes ma'am." He stood and bowed, his eyes merry. "You're a bold little thing, aren't you?"

Chapter Seven

The Teacher

I STOOD UP TO LEAVE. Captain Griffith said, "Try not to worry. God is on our side."

Papa always said God is on the side of the strongest army, but since I was working on becoming more tactful, all I said was, "I hope so."

The captain opened the door for me. I stood on the sunny street, thinking what to do. Papa might not be home for days. We couldn't go on alone in our dreary house, eating nothing but potatoes and jam. Perhaps someone would take us in.

There was Mrs. Miles, although I was still cross with her for breaking her promise to look after us. Neither had she been any help in getting us off Terrapin Island. But she had been my mother's dearest friend. Surely she would help us now, even if Mr. Miles had taken to his bed.

I found her house and knocked on the door. After a long time it opened, and a woman, white-haired and skinny as a buggy whip, peered out. "What do you want?"

"Is Mrs. Miles at home?"

"She is, but she's not receiving callers."

"Oh, I'm not a caller. I'm Susanna Simons. From Terrapin Island. Please ask her if I may come in. It's important."

"Just a minute."

It seemed forever before Mrs. Miles came to the door. "Susanna. I wasn't expecting you."

"I'm sorry. I'm in a desperate fix. Papa still isn't home and the boys and I—"

"Not home? How'd you get here?"

"We came on the flatboat."

"Merciful heavens! Come in and tell me all about it."

The woman with white hair was in the parlor. Mrs. Miles said, "This is my cousin Emma. There are three more just like her upstairs. I'd offer you some tea, but the servants have all left."

"Ours, too."

Mrs. Miles clicked her tongue. "It's disgraceful. After we clothed and fed them and took care of them for generations. Well, it's done now. I suppose we should be grateful they didn't kill us all. Tell me, how in the world did you get here on a flatboat? Why didn't you take the ferry?"

"It stopped running. By the time we got there, a sign was posted and there was no other way off the island."

"Merciful heavens!" she said again. "Whatever is keeping your father? I thought he was due back by now."

"That's why we're in trouble. We're all alone. May we stay here with you until he comes back? We won't be any bother."

She sighed and fussed with her skirt. "I'd help you if I could. But I'm afraid it's just not possible. Last night Emma and her sisters arrived, unannounced and un-invited, I might add. Afraid to stay in the country with the Yankees on the loose. So now I have four extra mouths to feed, the children to look after, and my poor husband has taken to his bed. Hasn't spoken a word since we got off the ferry. And not one servant around to help. It's all too much to bear."

"I could look after the children. I've had plenty of practice."

"I'm afraid not," Mrs. Miles said. "We're short of beds as it is."

"We'll sleep on the floor. We don't mind."

"Susanna. I appreciate your problem. Truly I do. But I'm afraid it's out of the question. I'm sorry."

Too angry for tears, I stood up. "I thought you were our friend! I thought you'd . . . oh, never mind! I'll ask Mrs. Pearson. Or Mrs. Ellis."

Mrs. Miles said, "If only you could. But Cynthia Ellis has gone to Atlanta to stay with her husband's people. And the Pearsons packed up and moved to Texas. Lock, stock, and barrel."

"Then what shall we do?"

"There's always the orphans' home."

"We're not orphans!"

"I know that! Don't get so upset. I'm only trying to help."

"If you really wanted to help, you'd take care of us, no matter what!"

"Well!" Mrs. Miles stood up. "There's no need to be rude! Yours is not the only life that's been turned upside down. You'd do well to remember that."

"But you said if I needed anything I should ask you!"

"I know what I said. But things have turned out much worse than I ever imagined." She followed me to the door. "Perhaps I can look in on you in a few days, when all this commotion dies down."

The door clicked shut behind me. I leaned against the cold iron gate. Papa always called me wise beyond my years, but I didn't feel wise; I felt small and alone. What good were friends if they wouldn't help you when you needed them? Mrs. Miles was just like Elias, pretending to be one thing when she was really another.

Wasn't there anyone left who would come to our aid? I thought of Miss Hastings, the headmistress at the School for Young Ladies. Perhaps she'd think me too bold for asking such an enormous favor, but she was my last hope.

The walk to her house was a short one. I knocked at the door. It opened, and the sight of dear Miss Hastings, so calm and smiling, reduced me to tears.

"Susanna! What is it, my dear?"

"I . . . we . . . I . . ."

"Well, whatever it is, it can't be as bad as all that. Come in and have some tea. We'll sort it out."

Then I related our recent troubles, including my visit to Mrs. Miles. "She won't take us in. And everyone else we know has left town. We need someone to look after us until Papa comes back."

"I see." Her blue eyes were serious and kind all at the same time. "I'm afraid I haven't any spare room either. My parents have taken over the second floor, and my two aunts from Georgia moved in recently. I myself am now sleeping in the attic."

"We wouldn't be a bit of trouble," I said. "We could sleep in the kitchen, or in the wash house. I could help you with the chores around here. Neddie, too. And I'll make Sammy behave. You'll see."

I waited anxiously while Miss Hastings refilled our cups. Then she said, "It wouldn't work, Susanna. Mother has always been a bit nervous, and this war has made everything worse. Besides, you can't sleep in the wash house, for goodness sake. It's full of spiders and who knows what else."

"I don't care! Anything is better than being alone and afraid. Please, Miss Hastings. Please let us stay. I've no one else to ask."

"I realize that." She frowned in the way that meant she was thinking very hard. "Perhaps there is something I can do to help."

"Truly?"

"I've been thinking of opening the school again. Not for the money of course, but to be useful. We could hold classes right here and invite all the planters' children."

"Even boys?" Neddie would be delighted, but convincing Sammy to attend would be a trial.

"Even boys. It's time Sammy got serious about his studies. There's the youngest Miles boy. He must be six or seven by now. And the Hamilton girls are back in the city. I saw them yesterday."

While I was still thinking about it, she said, "It isn't what you hoped for, but perhaps it will make things easier. And you're welcome to take your supper here. It's only for a short while anyway."

"Captain Griffith promised to send a message right away."

"If Captain Griffith made you a promise, you may be sure he'll keep it." She blushed and smiled to herself. "Tell you what. I'll see what books I can find, and we'll begin on Monday. That should give Sammy a few days to get used to the idea."

"All right. Thank you, Miss Hastings."

"I'm only sorry I can't do more. Come here on Monday at nine. We'll get started."

Standing on the street again, I felt almost happy. Captain Griffith was sending a message to Papa. And we would have school, and a good supper each night until Papa's return. Passing the confectioner's shop, I thought of Sammy. One bag of lemon drops wouldn't cost much. And a sweet would lift all our spirits.

The shop smelled of cinnamon and chocolate. I expected to find Mr. Perkins behind the counter. Instead, a strange woman gazed at me over the top of her spectacles. "Are you just looking, or do you want something?"

"A bag of lemon drops, please."

While she scooped the candies, I asked, "Where's Mr. Perkins?"

"Same place as most every other man. Off to join the army." She folded the top of the paper bag. "So then he sends word to me, clear to Baton Rouge, to come and keep his store open. Well, he was a good brother to me when my husband died, so I reckon I owed him a favor, even if he is a fool for toting a gun at his age. Anything else?"

"No, that's all."

"How about these last two chocolates? They're going stale, so you might as well take them. No sense throwing them out."

"All right then. Thank you."

She put the chocolates into another bag. I paid for the lemon drops and hurried home.

The boys were in the parlor, sitting cross-legged on the carpet. They were wearing turbans made of blue rags, and Neddie was waving the fireplace poker as if it were a magic wand. Sammy was holding one of the oil lamps.

Before I could speak, Neddie stood up and bowed. "It's Princess Susanna, returning to the palace of the great Simoni, king of all India."

Solemn as a preacher, Sammy bent over till his forehead touched the floor. "Welcome, beautiful princess."

Then he toppled over in a fit of giggles.

"What are you doing, Neddie?" I dropped my things on the chair.

"I am not Neddie, O beautiful princess. I am the great Simoni. Would you like to ride on my magic carpet?"

It seemed so long since we'd felt like a game of make-believe that I decided to play along. Soon enough, they would ask about Papa. "Thank you, great Simoni. Where are we going?"

"To see the Taj Mahal. The most beautiful building in all of India. Except for my palace, of course."

Sammy passed his hand over the lamp. "Away, magic carpet!"

Neddie waved the fireplace poker. "Behold, the Taj Mahal. Over there are the lovely gardens, and down that way are the marble fountains. Notice how they gleam in the sun."

"It's lovely, great Simoni," I said. "But I'm getting quite dizzy. Could we land the carpet now?"

"As you wish, O princess." He waved the poker again.

"What's in the bag?" Sammy asked. "Is it for me?"

"It's a surprise."

Neddie understood at once. "Papa isn't here."

"No."

Setting aside the lamp, Sammy took off his turban, glaring at me as if I were the one responsible for the war and all its misery. Neddie took off his turban, too. The poker rolled across the floor.

"But I've sent him a message," I said. "As soon as he receives it, he'll come straight home."

"When will that be?" Sammy asked. "He's been gone forever. I miss him."

"I don't know, Sam. Maybe in a week, if he's not too far away."

"Another week!" Sammy threw himself down and folded his hands over his chest, like a corpse in a coffin. "I'll be dead from your terrible cooking long before then."

Neddie poked Sammy's stomach. "Relax, Sam. You've got blubber to spare."

"Blubber?" Sammy sat up. "I'm not fat."

"Didn't say you were," Neddie said mildly. "But don't criticize Susanna's cooking unless you want to take over the job."

I opened the lemon drops. Sammy seized a handful. Neddie squeezed his wrist till Sammy yelped, "Let go!"

"No, you let go, Sammy! You're taking more than your share."

"How do you know? You didn't even count them!" Sammy appealed to me. "Make him turn loose, Susanna."

"Here. Give them to me. We'll count them right now."

There were four for each of us. Sammy ate his all at once, then reached for the other bag. "Whaz in 'ere?"

"Don't talk with your mouth full," Neddie said. "It's not polite." He put a lemon drop on the end of his tongue and closed his eyes while it melted.

"These are chocolate drops," I said. "But there are only two, so we have to share."

"I want my bite first," Sammy said.

"No you don't!" Neddie said. "You'll take the biggest piece."

"I will not!"

"Will too."

Their endless quarrels were driving me to distraction. Then I remembered something Papa had done one Christmas when Neddie and I argued over the last orange. I said to Sammy, "Where's your knife?"

"My pocket."

"All right. You may cut the chocolate in two."

His smile spread out slowly, like spilled milk. "Goody!"

"And then Neddie may choose which piece he wants."

Neddie said, "Fine with me."

Sammy took his time dividing the chocolates. Presently he looked up from his work. "Hey, Susanna. If I cut both pieces in half, and we each eat one, there'll be one piece left. Whose is that?"

"So many questions, Sammy!"

"It should be mine," Sammy said. "'Cause I'm the baby of the family."

Neddie snorted. "The last time I called you the baby of the family, you punched me."

"That was different." Sammy drew his knife through the candy.

"Susanna should have the extra piece," Neddie said. "For taking care of us."

But I let them share it while I told them about Miss Hastings and the school. Neddie's eyes positively glowed at the prospect of so many books, but Sammy balked. "Miss Hastings? That's a school for *girls!* I'm not going!"

"Fine," I said. "You don't have to. You can stay here alone all day. And when Papa comes home, you can tell him how you wouldn't mind me, even though he told you to, and why you want to grow up dumb as a post. And right after that, you can tell him what you'd like for Christmas. Then watch and see how many presents you get."

"That's not fair. That's blackmail!"

"I know."

Sammy sighed. "All right. I'll go. But I'm not singing any of those stupid songs. And I'm not going to dress up either."

"You don't have to," I told him. "It won't be so bad. Stephen is invited. And Miss Hastings is the finest teacher in the world. You'll like school. I promise."

"It won't be for long anyway," Sammy said. "When Papa comes back, we'll go back to Oakwood and Neddie and I will go riding and fishing again."

I didn't remind him that by now the Yankees were probably swarming over Terrapin Island. The boys went outside to play in the garden.

From my window I watched the clouds curling like fleece against the sky, my thoughts on dreadful Cousin Hettie. The year I was eight, she came to stay at Oakwood because our mother was too sick to care for us. She arrived on the train from Savannah, smelling of camphor and garlic. A more disagreeable woman I had never met. She rarely smiled. She scolded Papa for teaching me medicine, declaring that it was indecent. Noise made her nervous. Every time the boys laughed, she shushed them.

To keep us quiet one day, she showed us how to make holes in the ends of an egg and blow the insides out till all that was left was the shell.

That was how I felt now. Empty and fragile as an eggshell. Another week without Papa seemed like forever. I wanted to be courageous and dutiful for his sake, but I didn't feel the least bit brave. Tears bubbled in my throat, salty and hot.

"Please, Papa," I whispered. "Please come home."

Chapter Eight

The School

WHEN MONDAY CAME, we went to Miss Hastings's for school. Besides the three of us, there were Stephen Miles and the Hamilton girls, Elizabeth and Caroline, and two girls from St. Helena Island, Marie and Jane. There was a boy about Sammy's age, with curly black hair and eyes the color of the pine trees that grew on our island. Miss Hastings introduced him. "This is Jeremy O'Brien. He'll be studying with us for a while."

Caroline said, "I've never seen you before. Have you always lived here?"

"No," Jeremy said. "I came here this summer."

"Jeremy is staying at the orphans' home," Miss Hastings explained, "until they find his aunt Lucinda. Then he'll be going to live with her in Atlanta."

"What's an orphan?" Stephen asked.

"I know," Jane said. "It's somebody who doesn't have any parents, isn't it, Miss Hastings?"

"That's right."

82

"What happened to yours?" Stephen asked.

Miss Hastings said, "Perhaps Jeremy would rather not speak of it."

"I don't mind, ma'am." Jeremy turned to Stephen. "My ma died of typhoid some years back. Pa died fighting with General Beauregard at Manassas."

Everyone stared at Jeremy, awed and respectful, but a feeling of uneasiness swept over me. If Papa died helping General Lee, the boys and I would be orphans, too. Just like Jeremy.

Miss Hastings said, "All right, everyone. Let's begin."

At that moment, the door opened and Ellen Rinehart swept in like a princess arriving at a ball. I wished she hadn't come. She hated to study, and she was a terrible gossip. All she cared about was who had bought a new bonnet and who was getting married. We had never been true friends, but she took my arm and said, "Why, Susanna Simons! Here you are back in Charleston and you haven't even bothered to call on me. And me with hardly anyone left to talk to! You're a mean old thing!"

"Please sit down, Ellen," Miss Hastings said. "You're just in time for morning prayers."

Miss Hastings prayed for the safety of all our soldiers and for a swift end to the war. I prayed for Papa to come back. Then Miss Hastings handed out our books.

My assignment was history. Opening to the first chapter, I read about Nathan Hale, a hero of the American Revolution. He was a teacher who kept a school while spying on the British. When his deception was discovered, the British captured him and hanged him, without so much as a trial. Now Papa was spying, too, just like Nathan Hale. What would happen if the Yankees should discover his true intent?

The weight of Papa's secret and my own fear built up inside me like steam in a kettle.

"What's the matter, my dear?" Miss Hastings asked. "Is there anything I can do?"

Her kindness brought me perilously close to tears. And I did not want to weep. Not with Ellen there to see. If I did, everyone in town would know all about it before suppertime.

"Come with me."

Then, in the privacy of the hallway, the tears came over me. Miss Hastings didn't speak but made soothing noises till I was quiet again.

"I can appreciate how difficult this must be for you," she said, handing me a handkerchief. "It must be frightening not to know where your father is or when he might return."

"It's awful. Most of our friends have left town. I'm so useless in the kitchen I can barely boil water. And I'm worried about Papa. I can't do it anymore. It's too hard."

She sat on a green velvet chair beside the window. "No one so young should have so much responsibility, but honestly, Susanna, you're doing quite well." Outside, a mockingbird sang and a wagon rattled past. "You got your brothers off Terrapin Island safely. Now you're caring for them in that big house all by yourself. You even managed to persuade Sammy Simons to attend school. How you achieved *that*, I'll never know."

Her little speech lifted my spirits. I wiped my eyes.

"Your father will return safely. Until he does, you must find the courage to carry on."

"I'll try."

"I know you will. And now I have a surprise for you. The Confederate Ladies' Aid Society is planning a Christmas dance to raise money for the army. There will be music, of course, and lovely decorations. I realize you're a bit young, but Ellen is coming, and I think you should, too."

"A dance?"

Miss Hastings laughed. "Don't look so horrified. Why, one would think I'd asked you to swallow a worm."

"I'd rather eat a whole bucket of worms than go to a dance."

"Don't be silly. You'll have fun. And it's high time you started practicing the social graces."

Inside my head, I lined up all my excuses like a row of soldiers. "I wouldn't feel right, going to a dance with Papa away."

"It's for a good cause," Miss Hastings said. "I'm certain he'd approve."

"What about Neddie and Sammy? I couldn't leave them alone."

"Of course not. Your father may be home by then, but if not, my mother will watch over them. I've already asked her."

"I have nothing to wear. Most of my things are at Oak-wood."

"That shouldn't stop you. Everyone is wearing last year's fashions anyway. If this blockade goes on much longer, we'll all be wearing homespun. Don't worry. We'll find something."

"I'm not a very good dancer. I'd break everyone's toes."

"We'll practice after school. It's not hard."

She was trying to be kind, trying to take my mind off Papa and all my troubles. But the mere thought of dressing up and dancing in a room full of strangers made my stomach churn.

"Just give it a try," Miss Hastings said. "If you find it unbearable, I'll send you home early. I promise."

Papa would expect me to be a lady. Refusing the invitation after Miss Hastings had gone to so much trouble would be rude. "Thank you. I'll come."

"Splendid! We'll have a wonderful time." She stood up. "Don't forget, we're expecting you and your brothers for supper tonight. For now, we'd better get back to the children. It's much too quiet in there."

In our makeshift classroom, Neddie was sprawled on the floor, lost in Mr. Dickens's new book. Ellen was fussing with her hair combs, her book unopened at her feet. Jeremy and Sammy were helping Stephen draw a map of Europe. The little girls were having a pretend tea party.

"Good morning, Caroline." Jane sipped from an imaginary tea cup. "And how are you this fine morning?"

"Just terrible!" Caroline waved a fan she'd made from a piece of folded paper. "All my servants have run away. Whatever shall I do?"

At the end of the day, after our readings and recitations, Miss Hastings said, "Pay attention, everyone. Here's a question for you. Who knows what a marsupial is?"

"I know!" Neddie's hand shot up. "It's an animal with a pouch, like a kangaroo."

Ellen rolled her eyes. "Why, Neddie Simons! If you aren't just another Noah Webster. Tell me, do you know everything in the whole world?"

"Not yet," Neddie said. "But I'm working on it."

Miss Hastings said, "Tomorrow we'll have a visitor. He's bringing a marsupial with him."

Sammy looked up from his drawing. "Is he bringing a kangaroo?"

"Not a kangaroo, but an animal that lives right here in South Carolina. See if you can think tonight about what it might be. Tomorrow we'll find out if you're right. That's all for today."

Taking my arm as if we were the best of friends, Ellen said, "Have you ever heard of anything so ridiculous? Who cares about smelly old animals, for heaven's sake."

"I think they're interesting."

"You would! All you think about is riding that horse of yours or fishing in that smelly old river. What you should be thinking about is catching a husband. Eliza Ashworth got engaged last week, and she's barely fifteen. Her aunt gave a tea for her. It was divine. Strawberries and chocolates and the prettiest little iced cakes you ever saw."

"I like fishing. I'd rather be outdoors any day than stuck at a boring tea party."

"Fiddlesticks! The sun simply ruins one's complexion. If you find yourself without suitors someday, don't say I didn't warn you."

We said goodbye to Miss Hastings and went outside. All the boys had gathered at the gate, watching our soldiers practice their drills in the park across the street.

Ellen said, "I must go. But I'm truly glad you're back. You simply can't imagine how awful it's been here. Half our friends have left town and the other half are so scared they won't even poke their noses out the door. I am bored to tears! Oh, say you'll come to tea soon."

"I'll try."

I called to Neddie and Sammy and we started for home. At the corner, we bade goodbye to Stephen and Jeremy and turned up the street. Neddie lagged behind Sammy and me.

"Hey, Neddie," Sammy called. "I'll race you home."

"You go on," Neddie said. "I don't feel like it."

I waited till he caught up to us. "Are you all right?"

"I guess so."

Sammy said, "Guess what? Jeremy O'Brien hates the orphans' home."

"I don't suppose it would be much fun."

"He says they have about a million rules and if you break even one, you get punished."

"Sounds dreadful. Maybe they'll find his aunt soon, and he can live in Atlanta."

"If he doesn't go to Atlanta, can he spend Christmas with us?" Sammy asked. "He won't be any trouble. I promise. You'll hardly know he's there."

"Oh, Sammy. I can't think about that now. Let's wait to see if Papa is home by then, all right? Then we'll decide."

When we reached Meeting Street, our path was blocked by a group of men standing on the corner.

"It's true!" said one, waving his cigar in the air. "I have it on good authority. The Yankees are sending their gunboats up Broad River to Mackay's Point, and then straight to Coosawhatchie."

"What for?" said another. "There's nothing there but the fort and the train depot."

"Precisely," said the cigar man. "From there our soldiers can move in either direction. The Yankees would like nothing better than to blow up the railroad and invade Charleston. Then they'd have us cut off by land *and* sea."

The third one said, "Even so, they won't reach the fort for a while yet. It'll take some time for those Yankee tenderfoots to make their way that far upriver."

"True enough," the cigar man said, blowing out a puff of smoke. "With all the inland passages closed, they'll be forced to travel the backcountry. If we're lucky, the 'gators will eat 'em all before they get within ten miles of there."

The men laughed, but all their talk about Yankee invasions only increased my worry. I took Sammy's hand and we continued on toward home.

"Hey, Susanna. Guess why they named that train station Coosawhatchie. 'Cause it sounds like a steam engine. Listen." Sammy made a fist and moved his arm around and around, like train wheels. "*Coosa*-whatchie, *coosa*-whatchie, *coosa*-whatchie."

Sammy could always lift my spirits. "Did you like school today?"

"Yep. I like Miss Hastings."

"I knew you would."

He stopped in the street. "I'm going straight to Papa's library when we get home. I'll bet I'm the first one to figure out the mars . . . mars . . ."

"Marsupial."

The moment we arrived, Sammy turned toward Papa's library. Neddie came in and went past me without a word.

"What's the matter, Neddie?" I asked.

"My stomach hurts."

"You'll feel better after a proper supper."

"No. I don't feel like eating."

I touched his forehead. His skin was hot and damp. "You're sick," I said. "Why didn't you tell me?"

"You've got too much to worry about already."

"Go right to bed. I'll be there in a minute." I searched the medicine chest we'd brought from Oakwood and the cabinet in Papa's office, but there was nothing for the fever. No castor oil, no calomel, no quinine. There was nothing but blackberry bark and the last of the powdered alum. After Neddie drank the tea I'd brewed from the bark, I opened all the windows. Despite the cool breeze blowing in off the water, his condition grew worse.

"Sammy, come up here!"

He dashed up the stairs. "Guess what? I found—"

"Not now. Neddie's sick. Go find Dr. Scott. His house is on Friend Street. Near the Mileses' house."

"I know where it is."

"Tell him Neddie has a fever."

A look of pure terror stole into Sammy's eyes. One of Kit's sons had died of the fever the previous spring and had been carried off our island on a raft. For weeks afterward, Sammy fought sleep, fearing he would never wake.

Now I said, "I don't think it's the summer fever. But Neddie needs medicine."

"I'll be right back." He raced down the stairs. The front door slammed shut behind him.

Neddie moaned and licked his lips. I tried to stay calm, but worry coiled inside me like a snake. On rounds with Papa, I'd seen more than one person who'd felt right as rain in the morning and was dead by nightfall. Some fevers could take a person just like that.

Waiting for Sammy to fetch the doctor, I hovered over Neddie's bed. He looked so small and helpless lying there, his thin brown fingers curled on the blanket. From the very beginning, he'd been my strongest ally, my heart's own treasure.

"Oh, Neddie!" My tears spilled onto his pillow. "Don't you dare leave me now. I need you!"

From the street below came the murmur of voices and gentle laughter. The bells at St. Michael's rang. A train whistle shrieked.

At last, the door opened. Sammy pounded up the stairs. "How is he?"

"Worse. Where's Dr. Scott?"

"Gone out to the Carltons'. Their baby's real sick. But his wife sent this. She says it's all she can spare."

Pulling the stopper from the brown bottle, I tasted. "Quinine! Thank goodness!"

Taking care not to spill a single drop, I measured out the medicine. We roused Neddie and he swallowed it. His eyes fluttered. Then he lay back against the pillows.

"Is Neddie going to die?"

"I don't know. I pray not."

Sammy's face crumpled. "Where's Papa? I'm scared."

"Me, too, but we must be brave for Neddie's sake."

That night, we took turns bathing Neddie's face. In the morning Dr. Scott finally arrived. He wanted to treat Neddie with leeches, to draw out the fevered blood, but I refused. Papa had long ago abandoned such notions as old-fashioned and unreliable. Instead, I continued with the cold water baths and the quinine, through days and nights that, without Papa to comfort and guide me, seemed endless, each one harder to bear than the one before. Sammy and I slept on the floor beside Neddie's bed, our other worries all but forgotten as we waited to see whether Neddie would get well.

Chapter Nine

The Dance

AFTER FOUR DAYS, the fever broke, and my spirits soared. When Neddie was strong enough, we continued at school with Miss Hastings. Then he caught a dreadful cold, and the fever came back worse than ever. Coming out of Mr. Miller's store one day, near despair because the quinine was gone, I saw Captain Trimble in the street, and he said he'd heard Papa was on his way to Charleston. My heart nearly bursting, I ran all the way home to tell the boys the happy news. But it wasn't true. Twice I went to army headquarters to inquire about Papa, but Captain Griffith's reply was always the same. Wait.

The day of the dance arrived and still Papa hadn't returned. After Sammy and I finished breakfast, I took a tray to Neddie's room. Almost two weeks had passed since he'd caught cold. He was much better, but this time I'd insisted he stay in bed until he was completely well.

When I came in, he set aside his book. "Tonight's the big night. Your first grown-up dance."

"I'm going only to please Miss Hastings. I don't know why she and Papa are so determined to reform me."

"Maybe it won't be as bad as you think. Just try to have fun, Susanna. You deserve it. You've been doing all the work around here."

"Sammy's been a big help. He hasn't even complained about school."

"Why should he, as long as he has Jeremy for a play-mate." Neddie picked up his spoon. "Besides, they haven't been studying all that hard. Yesterday they went fishing in Jeremy's boat."

"I didn't know he had one."

"He does. Dandy little rowboat, Sammy says. They keep it tied in the cove out beyond the docks."

"Sammy should have asked my permission. The water's deep down there."

"Only at high tide. Sammy said they were playing pirates with Stephen last night."

"All the same, he shouldn't go without asking me."

Neddie licked his spoon. "All set for the dance?"

"I suppose. Miss Hastings is lending me a dress. And her mother is coming to stay with you till I get back. Do you want anything else?"

"Nope. I'm going to catch up on the schoolwork I've missed." The clock in the hallway bonged. "You'd better get going. I heard it takes nearly all day for a girl to get dressed for a dance."

"I shouldn't wonder. All those ridiculous hoops and petticoats. They're such a bother!"

He grinned. "Some girls enjoy it!"

Because of the dance there was no school, so I passed the morning dusting the parlor and helping Sammy with his arithmetic. Then Miss Hastings's mother arrived. Her name was Mrs. Willis, because Mr. Hastings had died of the summer fever, and then she'd married Mr. Willis.

She marched into the parlor and handed Sammy a book. "Here. Find a corner somewhere and don't make any noise. My head hurts."

Settling into Papa's favorite chair, she opened a big bag. "Might as well finish rolling these bandages. Well, run along, Susanna. Don't keep Miss Hastings waiting."

I sent Sammy my special look. The one that said, "mind your manners."

"We'll get on, so long as he's quiet," Mrs. Willis said. "Go on now. Don't be late."

Miss Hastings was watching for me at the window. She opened the door, her words tumbling out. "Come in! Your dress is all ready. I'm afraid the color is a bit summery for this time of year, but everyone's in the same boat, after all. Once you're dressed, I'll be up to do your hair. Just go on up, dear."

In a tiny room under the eaves, I undressed and left my everyday clothes on the chair. The dress I was to wear was an old-fashioned one with bits of embroidery on the sleeves and a sky blue skirt edged with miles of white lace. I fastened hoops at my waist, pulled the dress over my head, and settled the skirt over them. It swayed like an enormous bell.

Presently Miss Hastings came in to do up the row of buttons in the back. "I was hoping this dress would fit you," she said. "My father brought it from Paris the year I turned thirteen. He said the color matched my eyes." She brushed out my braids and fashioned a crown of curls on top of my head. Our eyes met in the mirror. "There. You see? Pretty as a picture. I wish your father could see you."

My cheeks went warm, though, of course, I wasn't pretty as a picture. I was just a plain girl in a fancy dress, a stranger to myself.

Miss Hastings dabbed perfume behind my ears. "Time to go. We mustn't keep Captain Griffith waiting."

Soon his carriage arrived and we started for the dance. Above the clopping of the horses' hooves, Miss Hastings said, "Our committee is delighted that so many people are coming tonight. We should raise a lot of money for the army."

"Your gracious influence, Miss Hastings, will undoubtedly contribute much to the success of the evening," the captain said, smiling down at her.

"Such lavish praise, Captain." Her face turned pink. "I did less than I should have, but Susanna and I have been busy at school, haven't we, dear?"

Captain Griffith said to me, "I've been away for three days, so I haven't any word of your pa. But the troops from Florida have arrived, including a couple of doctors."

"Why that's wonderful news, isn't it?" Miss Hastings said. "Surely now General Lee will send your father home."

The carriage halted. Captain Griffith helped us alight, and we entered the hall.

It looked like a picture in a storybook. The tables were set with white cloths and bowls of pink flowers, and hundreds of glittering candles. There were wreaths of grapevine and ivy and clumps of mistletoe tied with white ribbons. In one corner stood a Christmas tree, shiny with red garlands and silver bells. The smells of pine needles and ladies' sachets and cologne water all mixed together in the air.

The doors at the far end of the hall opened, and a group of girls rustled in on a blast of winter wind.

"Watch out," Miss Hastings whispered. "Here comes Ellen."

"Susanna!" Ellen kissed my cheek. "Is that you? Why, you look absolutely divine! You see what a girl can do when she really tries?" Her peacock-feather fan swished back and forth. "Guess what? The most delicious bit of gossip! I heard it just this afternoon. They say . . ."

"Ellen!" someone called. "Come and taste this heavenly punch!"

"Coming!" She turned back to me. "I'll tell you later. You simply won't believe it. Why, I had to hear it from at least three people before it even began to seem real."

Then the soldiers arrived. Some wore new uniforms, some wore sashes and sabers. The Confederate ladies introduced everyone and it was time for the first dance.

I stood there, wishing with all my heart that I'd never come. Suppose I stepped on someone's feet? Suppose I couldn't think of a single intelligent thing to say?

Then Captain Griffith bowed over my hand. "May I have this dance?"

At first my legs felt stiff as sticks, and every time I turned, my skirt bumped into something. I counted *one-two-three* inside my head, the way I'd practiced with Miss Hastings. Captain Griffith kept on nodding and smiling, his eyes so full of kindness that I soon felt less afraid. When the music stopped, he bowed again and went in search of Miss Hastings.

Then another soldier said, "Miss Simons. Miss Hastings gave me permission to speak to you. I'm John Chapin. May I have this dance?"

In his new uniform, he looked like a boy playing dress up, someone scarcely older than Neddie. The mere thought of my dear brother going off to battle made me shiver.

"Are you cold?" John asked. "I'll be happy to fetch your wrap."

"No thank you." We swayed and turned. "I was just wondering about something."

"What?"

"How old are you?"

He laughed. "You don't mince words, do you? As a matter of fact, I turned sixteen last Saturday."

"That's awfully young to be in the army."

"And you're awfully young to be at such a grown-up affair. Why, I'll bet you're not a day over fifteen."

Then I dared not reveal my true age. Round and round we turned, my skirt whispering on the polished floor. The music and flowers and the flickering candles were so beautiful that for a moment my spirits lifted, all my misfortunes forgotten.

When at last the music stopped, Miss Hastings called to me and said, "I see you've met John. Did he tell you he's my cousin? From Atlanta. We see far too little of him these days, I'm afraid."

Then Miss Lovejoy, from the orphans' home, joined our circle. "Have you heard the news?"

My breath caught. Had something happened to Papa?

"It's Darcy Miles," she said. "Killed in Virginia. They just got word today."

For a moment we stood there in stunned silence, certain that it was all a dreadful mistake. Darcy was just a boy. He couldn't be dead.

"Oh, this is terrible!" Miss Hastings said. "That poor woman. First her husband's illness and now this."

Miss Lovejoy murmured a reply, but I was lost in memories of happy days with Darcy, digging for oysters in the mudflats, racing our horses along the road between Oakwood and Summerhill.

The music started again, sounding strange and far away. Captain Griffith said, "I know it seems heartless to go on dancing after such terrible news, but we're here to raise money for the army. We must carry on so that Darcy's death will not have been for nothing." He patted my shoulder. "Try to enjoy the rest of the evening, my dear."

"He's right," John said. "You mustn't dwell on it. There's nothing you can do."

"I promised to write to him, but we left home so quickly, I didn't have the chance. And now it's too late."

"He would have understood," John said. "Listen. If you don't feel like dancing, we can talk. Cousin Sarah says you were responsible for getting your family off Terrapin Island."

"When the Yankees invaded Port Royal, we had no choice. We had to leave."

"Poor girl. You must have been scared out of your wits. But the war won't go on much longer. Once the rest of our troops reach Coosawhatchie, General Lee will—"

Coosawhatchie. The man with the cigar was right. General Lee *was* headquartered there and the Yankee gunboats were on their way upriver.

"Someone has to warn General Lee!" I said. "The Yankees plan to go there, to destroy the railroad."

"That old rumor's been around for weeks, but everybody knows the Yanks are headed south to wait for reinforcements."

"Perhaps they're saying that to fool General Lee. Someone should tell him what I heard. Just in case."

"If you'd been at HQ today, you could have told him yourself," John said. "He came in for an inspection this morning, and had supper at the Mills House. I hear he's leaving on the train tonight."

"He's *here?* I must speak to him."

"Don't be silly. The general's much too smart to credit street gossip."

"At least I can ask about my father. He should have been home weeks ago."

John took out his watch. "The train won't leave for a long time yet. Stay a little longer, and I'll escort you to the station myself."

"You promise?"

"I do. Look, the program's starting."

Some ladies arrived wearing fluffy white dresses that made them look like swans. They sang Christmas carols meant to make us happy, but my heart was burdened with grief. The music reminded me of last Christmas when Darcy spent the afternoon with us at Oakwood. Of course there'd been talk of the war that would surely follow our recent secession, but even that prospect hadn't dampened our merriment.

Now he was dead, and the music seemed too loud, the candles too bright. Miss Lovejoy and Miss Hastings were holding onto each other, weeping. I felt cold.

When the ladies finished singing, Mr. Miller began a speech. "Ladies and gentlemen. Today we have word that more troops are organizing to join in the defense of our great Confederacy. They will need blankets, weapons, and shoes."

Miss Hastings gave me a brave, sad smile and held my hand. Mr. Miller went on talking. "Supplying an army costs money. And while we've raised a good bit here tonight, it won't be nearly enough. We're asking for donations of money or other valuables you're willing to give to the cause."

Rings and watches, fancy ivory fans, gold coins and silver hair clips tinkled into the plates that were passed among us. Captain Griffith contributed his gold watch chain. Miss Hastings unfastened her silver necklace and dropped it into the plate.

Would you send more warm socks and some new boots? Remembering Darcy's letter to his mother, I felt guilty that I had nothing valuable to give.

The dancing began again, but I couldn't stop thinking about General Lee having supper a few streets away. Suppose the Yankees *were* planning to attack Coosawhatchie. If Papa were there, he might be killed or captured. But if he were on his way home, General Lee would know that, too, wouldn't he?

I had to see the general. He could laugh at me if he wished. It wouldn't matter. The only thing that mattered was having Papa home.

The band played "Dixie." Everyone began singing and clapping, too caught up in the music to notice as I slipped through the doors. A train whistle shrieked, echoing through the dark, empty streets. Gathering my skirts, I ran for the station, hoping to see General Lee before his train pulled away.

Chapter Ten

The Fire

THE TRAIN STATION was full of noise and confusion.
Dozens of people stood in line to buy tickets. On the platform, a jumble of bags and boxes and crates waited to be
put aboard. Hurrying through the crowd, I glanced at
each face, hoping to recognize General Lee from newspaper pictures or from the descriptions of him making the
rounds in town. Men said he loved a good story and was
every inch a soldier; ladies that he was the handsomest
man in the army.

From a group of Confederate soldiers at the far end of
the platform came a deep, rolling laugh. Someone said,
"That's a good one, General!"

My heart pounded in my ears. At long last, news of
Papa. Perhaps General Lee himself would ride out to a
hospital somewhere and give Papa my message. I imagined Papa hurrying straight home and all my worries
blowing away like feathers in the wind.

"All aboard!" the stationmaster called.

Like a minnow swimming against the current, I pushed toward the end of the platform. "Please! Wait!"

The doors to the train squeaked shut.

"General! Please!"

The train began to move. Ladies wept and jostled and called out their goodbyes, waving their handkerchiefs at the soldiers. With a final blast of the whistle, the train disappeared, its yellow lantern swaying in the darkness, taking with it the soldiers and all my dearest hopes.

I stood there, sick at heart. If only I'd left the dance sooner instead of wasting time behaving like a girl. Now my chance was lost.

The church bells tolled the hour. By now the dance was ending and Miss Hastings would be looking for me. Leaving the train station, I set off toward the great hall, past some people singing carols in the street, past a late-returning drayman in his empty wagon.

Without my shawl, I was soon numb with cold. Turning down a narrow alley, I stopped for a moment to warm myself in the shelter of the buildings before continuing on.

As I neared the great hall, a faint orange glow appeared in the sky, filling me with dread. Suppose the Yankee gunboats *were* firing on us after all. If that were true, no place would be safe.

The church bells clanged furiously. High in the steeple, a red lantern appeared. Then a terrifying sound, like the booming of cannon, set the ground beneath my feet to trembling.

People poured into the streets. Someone shouted, "There's a fire on East Bay!"

All notions of returning to the dance vanished. I turned and ran for home.

The fierce wind sent the fire jumping from street to street, curling over doorways and rooftops. One by one, houses and shops swayed and fell. The sound of it roared in my ears. The fire edged closer to our house. The smoke was black and thick with cinders. A great curtain of fire lit the street, bright as day. Houses popped and blazed. Dark, twisting shadows danced against the walls.

On the corner, a brigade of men with water buckets blocked my path. One of them pushed me back toward the sidewalk. "Here, miss. You can't go that way."

"My family!" I cried. But he'd already turned away.

I climbed a fence and raced down the alley, across lawns and gardens, through heavy gates that burned my fingers, at last reaching our back door. Breathless and shaking with fear, I rattled the lock and pounded on the door till at last Mrs. Willis threw it open.

"Are my brothers all right?" I asked. "Neddie! Where are you?"

"We've been on the roof, but the fire's coming this way," Mrs. Willis said. "It's time to go."

Pushing past her, I raced up the stairs and onto the roof, calling for my brothers.

When he saw me, Sammy began to cry. "Is it the Yankees?"

"I don't know!" I said. "But we have to run. Now!"

Yet as soon as we were inside, Neddie turned away and ran along the hallway.

"Where are you going?" I shouted.

"The cash box!" He dashed into my room and came running back. I pushed him ahead of me down the stairs. Mrs. Willis, holding her bag of bandages, hurried along behind us. Then the house across the street burst into flames with such force that the window in our front parlor shattered. Sammy screamed and covered his ears.

"Stop that!" Mrs. Willis caught Sammy's arms and held him fast. "This is no time for hysterics. I'll take you to my house. So long as the fire stays south, we'll be all right. Now stop whining."

I gave Sammy a quick hug. "It's all right. Hold my hand."

Like a pied piper, Mrs. Willis led us through the milling crowd. All along our way, burning timbers tumbled into the street.

Then Sammy yelled, "Susanna! Our house!"

I heard a loud whoosh as the roof caught fire, but I couldn't look back. My heart, too, burned with grief. Now we had no place where we belonged. Sammy clutched my hand. "Will we have to live at the orphans' home?"

"I don't know. We can't worry about it now. Come on."

From the safety of Mrs. Willis's house, we watched far into the night as the city burned. Sammy fell asleep on the floor in the parlor, but Neddie and I were still awake when Miss Hastings and Captain Griffith arrived, their clothes peppered with burn holes and blackened with soot.

"There you are, Susanna!" Miss Hastings said. "I've been frantic with worry. Why didn't you wait for me? I looked everywhere for you! Everywhere!" Her voice shook. "Half the town is gone. The Art Association is a ruin. The Rineharts, the Millers, the Rutledges all have lost their homes."

"Ours burned, too," Neddie said.

"Oh! I'm truly sorry." She dropped her cloak onto a chair. "It's nearly three o'clock. You children should sleep. There's nothing to be done."

Mrs. Willis made beds on the floor in the parlor for the boys. Miss Hastings led me to the room where I had dressed for the dance such a short time before. Without lighting the lamp, she opened a chest and took out blankets and a pillow. "I'm sorry the aunts have the bed. Will you be all right on the floor?"

Overcome with weariness and grief, I sank gratefully onto my makeshift bed. The last thing I heard before sleep came was the mournful peal of a church bell crashing onto the cobblestones.

When we woke the next day, Miss Hastings told us that Captain Griffith and his men had exploded fourteen houses on Queen Street to try to stop the fire. But despite such drastic measures, despite the rain that had fallen, the fire had raged on all night.

Neddie listened to the news with his head down, his boot tapping the carpet. For once, even Sammy was speechless.

Mr. Willis had gone out at first light to inspect the damage. Now he said, "I can't believe it, Sarah. This city is in ruins."

Miss Hastings perched on the arm of his chair. "What caused the fire, Pa? Was it the Yankees?"

Sammy said, "If it was, you just wait till my Papa gets back. He'll tear every one of them to pieces for burning down our house."

Mr. Willis said, "Folks want to blame it on the Yankees, but the authorities think it started down on Hasell Street. They say a family of slaves made a cooking fire and it got out of hand."

"You'd think they'd have more sense than to start a fire with a wind like we had last night," Miss Hastings said. "Now look at all the misery they've caused. As if this war is not misery enough."

"There now, dear," Mrs. Willis said. "No use working yourself into a state. You'll just upset the children."

Miss Hastings smiled bravely, but her chin quivered. I, too, was near tears. I wanted to feel normal again, to go to sleep at night feeling safe and wake up in the morning certain of what the day would bring. But that was like wishing for the moon.

Miss Hastings said, "Children, you mustn't be afraid. We'll be crowded, but you'll stay here until your father returns."

Neddie jumped up, his thin little face streaked with tears. "I wish everybody would stop talking about Papa's coming back! He's not." He glared at Sammy and me. "We're orphans. Just like Jeremy!"

Sammy burst into tears and hid his face in my skirts. For the first time since leaving Oakwood, I was truly furious with Neddie. "Now look what you've done!"

He ran outside, banging the door behind him.

"I'll see to him," Miss Hastings said.

But Mr. Willis stopped her. "Leave him alone, Sarah. He'll be all right."

Sammy tugged on my skirts. "Is Neddie telling the truth? Are we going to live in the orphans' home?"

"Of course not, you little goose."

"But what if Papa never comes back?"

"He will, as soon as he can. But if he's not back by Christmas, we'll send word to Cousin Hettie." Even as I said the words, I wasn't certain I could find her. Along with everything else, Papa's letter had burned.

"Do I know her?" Sammy asked. "Is she nice?"

"She came to Oakwood once, but you were only three years old. We painted some eggshells."

"Oh, I remember her!" Sammy's nose wrinkled like a rabbit's. "She was mean. And she smelled funny. I'd *rather* be an orphan."

Miss Hastings said, "Sammy. Enough of this gloomy talk. Of course your father will be back. And tomorrow we'll start school again. I'm not sure anyone else will come, but we'll feel much better if we have useful work to do."

"I don't want to." Sammy's bottom lip stuck out like a shelf. "I don't feel like working."

Miss Hastings's brows went up, a certain sign we were about to get one of her famous homilies. She had one for nearly any circumstance. "It is through work that one learns fidelity, Sammy. I won't have an idler under my roof."

"What's fidelity?"

"You'll just have to come to school tomorrow and find out," she said. "Meantime, we need breakfast. Go tell your brother he has ten minutes to make himself presentable. And no more tears. We will not feel sorry for ourselves."

A few minutes later, we crowded around a table laden with honey and grits and ham from the Willis's storehouse. There wasn't room for everyone, so the two aunts ate in their room beneath the eaves. Mr. and Mrs. Willis took their breakfast in the parlor. Though they were ever so polite, professing not to mind one bit, their smiles were stiff as Papa's Sunday shirt.

In the afternoon, Miss Hastings brought out her easel and paints and we took turns copying the picture of men and horses that hung above the mantel. Then, despite all our misfortunes, we sang some hymns while she played the piano.

After that, she sent us off to nap, but my bed of blankets was lumpy with worry. I thought about Papa, General Lee at Coosawhatchie, and our soldiers on their way to join him. How much was rumor and how much was truth? Were the Yankees waiting for more troops, as John Chapin had said, or were they on their way to destroy the railroad? It had been nearly a month since Captain Griffith had sent Papa my message, and we were still alone. Our house, all our worldly possessions, were gone, and my endless waiting had yielded nothing but more uncertainty and fear.

Then an idea captured my imagination. I would find General Lee and tell him what I'd heard. And I would find Papa and bring him home.

Chapter Eleven

Three Against the Tide

I SAT UP, planning everything out in my head. I would wait till evening, then leave a note saying that I was on an important errand. With money from the cash box, I'd buy a train ticket to Coosawhatchie. From there I could walk to General Lee's headquarters and tell him what I knew. And find Papa.

Once I'd decided to go, I felt tingly, as if ten thousand pins were pricking my skin. But the rest of the afternoon went by slowly, like a long sermon on a hot Sunday. I helped Miss Hastings hang out the wash and read another chapter in my history book. After supper, I started upstairs to get the money and write my note.

Upon reaching the landing, I heard Miss Hastings and her mother in the hallway just above my head. It was impossible not to hear their furious whispering.

" . . . all well and good to have school for them, but really,

Sarah, you mustn't turn these children into a lifelong project. It's too inconvenient having them eternally underfoot."

"What would you have me do, Mother? Toss them into the street?"

"Don't be ridiculous. I suppose there's nothing to be done for it now, but I certainly hope that father of theirs turns up soon."

"No more than they wish it, I'm sure!"

A door closed, and I heard no more. But now I was more determined than ever to find Papa.

I took the money and wrote my note, then waited for the boys to fall asleep. When at last the house grew quiet, I crept down the creaky servant's staircase and let myself out into the garden.

The air was bitter with smoke and ashes. Everywhere I looked were the burned-out shells of buildings. Like great tombstones, their brick chimneys stood, stark against the cold, black sky. In the dim light of the streetlamps, broken glass glittered. It crunched beneath my feet as I skimmed along the streets toward the depot.

The night train chuffed in. Taking up their boxes and trunks and crying children, the waiting passengers jostled onto the cars, pressing shoulder to shoulder in the aisles.

The agent closed the ticket window and wrote on his chalkboard: COME BACK TOMORROW. People grumbled and muttered and settled in for the night. I stood there thinking what to do.

There were so many people waiting for trains it might be days before I could leave. By then it could be too late. I thought of our flatboat waiting in the cove, but we had needed Elias to bring it safely down the river. Then I remembered Jeremy's rowboat. Small and lightweight, it would be perfect for traveling the shoals and inlets in the backcountry. Sooner or later I would reach the railroad, and it would lead me to General Lee.

To someone unfamiliar with that maze of creeks and shoals and rivers, such a journey might seem impossible. But I was a child of the tides and the marshes. The names of the rivers—Stono, Edisto, Ashepoo, Combahee—were as familiar to me as my own. Even if I hadn't known a single thing about them, I could not have abandoned my plan. For too long we'd depended on the kindness of others. We were without money, without a home, desperate with waiting. I felt like an army of one, fighting for the only thing that mattered: bringing Papa home.

I returned to Miss Hastings's house to get what I needed for the journey. Light glowed from the parlor window, but the house seemed quiet. In the garden, Mrs. Willis's old cat slid past my feet and disappeared into the lilac bushes. I peered into the darkness, scarcely believing my good luck. No one had remembered to take in the wash. Among the linens and skirts and tablecloths dangling from the clothesline were Mr. Willis's brown trousers. Of course they would be miles too big, but I could roll up the legs and belt them with my sash. Anything would be better than my skirts.

In the cookhouse were baskets of dried apples, part of a loaf of bread, and the ham left over from breakfast. After putting the food into a string bag, I went out to fill a water jar. With each of my movements the handle squeaked, but I dared not begin the journey without plenty of fresh water. A moment later a candle flickered behind a second-floor window. I hid in the shadows, holding my breath. If Miss Hastings caught me, I'd never have another chance to find Papa.

The light burned steadily near the window, then went out. Returning to the cookhouse, I changed into Mr. Willis's trousers, tucked in my bodice and cinched my sash, then pinned up my braids and buttoned my shoes. Keeping to the shadows, I went out the gate and hurried along the darkened streets, through the twisting alleyways and past the docks, hoping to find Jeremy's boat before the turning of the tide.

At the place where the docks ended, I followed a worn path until my foot hit something hard. Bending down, I felt around in the dark . My fingers closed over a clump of slick seaweed, a length of prickly rope stiff with salt, and then the smooth wood of the boat. After stowing my food bag in the bow, I bent to untie the line.

Above me, the weeds rustled and a voice whispered, "Susanna?"

"Neddie?"

He came through the tall grasses with Sammy.

"What are you doing here?" I straightened, still holding on to the line.

"What do you think?" Neddie asked. "We're coming with you." In the darkness, I could barely discern his features, but it was easy to imagine a determined scowl on his thin little face.

"We followed you," Sammy said. "We saw you sneaking out." He sounded excited, as if he were about to embark on a long-awaited adventure.

"Obviously. Both of you, go back to Miss Hastings's right this minute! And not one word about my being down here. Understand?"

Neddie tugged the line out of my hands. "Not unless you come back, too."

"I can't come," I said, trying to be patient when I really felt like shouting. "I have to see General Lee."

"You can't go alone," Neddie said. "What if you get sick or lost? You need me."

"Me too," Sammy said. "I'm a big help. You said so yourself."

"I know, Sammy, but—"

"We're coming," Neddie said stubbornly. "Either that or I'm telling Miss Hastings, and she'll send Mr. Willis after you. You won't get as far as Mosquito Creek."

I learned then that being on the receiving end of blackmail isn't pleasant. "Hurry up, then. The tide's turning."

Neddie untied the line and we got in the boat. It was quite stubby but steady on the tide. Removing his coat, Neddie secured it in the bow with the rope. Sammy settled in the stern. I pulled on the oars, and soon we cleared the cove. Behind us lay the skeletons of burned-out houses and the lights of the Yankee gunboats, shining on the water. A steady wind chilled our faces. Stars flickered in the cloudless sky.

When we reached deeper water at the mouth of the river, the incoming tide rushed against the bank and slid away again. We swirled back toward the cove, spinning like a leaf in a storm.

"Help me!" I shouted. Neddie and Sammy scrambled on to the seat beside me. Together they manned one oar and I took the other. The whoosh-whoosh of the water filled my ears.

The boat struck something in the water. The stern lifted into the air, throwing us off the seats. "Hold on!" Neddie yelled, and then the water closed over me, pulling me down. My lungs burned. I kicked my legs, pushing toward the surface.

My head struck the side of the boat and I came up gasping. "Neddie! Help me."

There was no answer. "Sammy!"

Both the boys were in the water. Diving beneath the boat, I swam in a wide circle, searching for them in the blackness. The cold numbed my arms and legs. The current pulled me farther from the boat. Then something brushed my leg. Grasping it for dear life, I kicked again and broke the surface.

"Sammy! Are you all right?"

"Where's Neddie?" His arms came around my neck.

"I don't know."

The boat had drifted away. We took turns calling for Neddie, clinging together in the black water.

"He's dead!" Sammy beat my chest with his fists, dragging us under.

"Stop it!" I held him fast, treading water. "Listen, Sam. We have to swim to shore. Can you do it?"

"We can't leave Neddie out here."

"We can't find him in the dark. We need help."

Then we heard a splashing sound and Neddie called, "Susanna?"

"Here!" We shouted and churned in the water, hoping Neddie could follow the sound.

A dark shape appeared, and then the bow of the boat struck my shoulder.

"Neddie! Are you all right?"

"Yes. Is Sammy with you?"

"I'm here!" Sammy said. "I'm freezing to death. Help me."

Neddie pulled Sammy over the side, then the boys helped me climb in. We sat for a moment, catching our breath, while the boat bobbed in the current. Then I took up the oars. Cold and tired though we were, there was no time to rest, and no one to come to our aid. There was only Sammy and Neddie and me. Three against the tide.

The boat swirled and dipped. Water splashed onto our shoes. With their hands and caps, the boys bailed while I rowed, my fingers on the oars frozen and brittle as sticks. Shivering in the cold, with only the stars to guide us, we at last left the city behind. Sammy dropped onto the bottom of the boat. "I'm too tired, Susanna. I can't do this anymore."

"Yes you can." Neddie helped him to his feet again. "You can't quit now."

We kept going until at last the river narrowed and the boat settled onto quiet water. The sky filled with pearly light, and ahead of us lay the slow brown waters of Mosquito Creek.

"We made it," Neddie said quietly.

For a while we drifted among the sea grasses and thick marshes, past flocks of egrets and solitary herons fishing in the misty shallows.

Sammy stretched and rubbed his eyes. "Holy smokes! Where'd you get those clothes?"

"Borrowed them from Mr. Willis. I'm going to take them back, though."

Neddie laughed and rubbed his hands against the morning chill. "They'll never be the same."

"You look like a boy," Sammy said. "What did you do to your hair?"

"Pinned it out of the way, if you must know. You have no idea how much bother it is being a girl."

"I'm hungry," Sammy announced. "What did you bring to eat, Susanna? I hope there's some ginger cake."

Fearing all my provisions lost, I felt beneath the seat till my fingers closed over the wet bag. "No ginger cake. There are apples and some ham, but we'll have to be careful. I didn't bring enough for three."

Neddie pulled his coat from the bow. "I brought some cheese and pickles and some carrots."

"Oh, good! Where'd you get all that?"

"I knew you'd clean out the cookhouse, so I looked in the pantry."

Then I remembered the light I'd seen in the window. "You spied on me!"

"I saw the note you left and figured you were going to find Papa. So Sammy and I watched till you left, then we sneaked out and followed you."

Despite everything, I was glad for their company. The journey to Coosawhatchie was a long one, and nighttime in the marshes could be scary.

"Tide's coming in," Neddie said. "We should go."

We set out again along the curving water, past yellow-green marshes and shiny mudflats. Above us, a flock of birds made a long, dark line in the sky. Sammy jumped onto the seat. "Look, Neddie! Pelicans! I bet there's about a million of them. I'll bet they—Oh!"

He stumbled and Neddie rushed to steady him, knocking the oar out of my hand. With a sickening lurch, the boat spilled us all into the water.

I came up just in time to see our food bag sinking to the bottom. "Creation! Now see what you've done!"

Sammy blew out a mouthful of brown water. "I'm sorry! I didn't do it on purpose!"

Neddie bobbed up beside me. "Help me turn the boat over."

We righted the boat and climbed in again. "Now what are we supposed to do?" I asked. "How could you be so careless, Sammy?"

"I said I was sorry."

"Sorry? You should have stayed with Miss Hastings. You're nothing but a nuisance! And don't you dare start crying. It won't do a bit of good!"

"Don't worry. We can find some food out here," Neddie said. "We've done it before."

"Yes, but we at least had a fishing line and matches for a fire."

From his inside pocket, Neddie drew out a tin box. "I never go anywhere without my matches."

"See?" Sammy said. "It's not so bad, Susanna. Maybe we can catch a fish."

"With our bare hands, I suppose!"

Neddie thought for a moment. "We could make a spear. I saw one in a book once."

"I brought my knife," Sammy said.

I huddled on the seat, cold, wet, and hungry, dismayed that my careful plan had gone so terribly wrong.

"It's not your fault," Neddie said. "We shouldn't have followed you. But we got scared, thinking about you out here all by yourself."

"Oh, Neddie. Perhaps I shouldn't have come, either, but it seems the only way to get Papa back. And I'm glad you're here. If only we had something to eat."

We came to a bend in the water. Neddie stood up in the boat. With Sammy's knife he cut a strong reed and sharpened the end. When it was finished, he waded into the shallows.

Silencing us with a finger to his lips, he drew back and drove the spear into the water. "Missed!"

He tried again. And again.

The sun dropped behind the trees. I shivered in my wet clothes.

"What's the matter, Neddie?" Sammy asked. "I thought your aim was better than that."

"I can't understand it. I must be doing something wrong."

Looking down into the murky water, Sammy said, "I wish there was more light so you could see better."

"Light!" Neddie's head came up. "Sammy, you're a genuine genius!"

Sammy blinked. "I am?"

"Susanna, remember the first day of school, when Miss Hastings showed us how light bends when it goes through water?"

"The stick in the water glass?"

"Yes. When we put the stick in the water, it looked broken. But it really wasn't. It must be the same with the fish. They're not where they seem to be. I should aim farther down. Below them."

We waited for more fish, Sammy and I in the boat, Neddie in the shallows. At last, Neddie drew back and plunged his spear into the water again. And missed again.

"Drat!" Sammy muttered.

Then Neddie tried once more and came up with a silvery fish, twisting on the spear. "Got one!"

"It's about time," Sammy said. "Let's eat. I'm about to perish!"

"Hold your horses," Neddie said. "We need more than one old fish."

But it seemed the fish had learned a lesson, too. They disappeared into the long shadows. At last Neddie gave up and climbed back into the boat.

Ebb tide began. Birds settled into the trees. The last weak rays of sunlight unfolded like a red blanket. We stopped for the night and roasted the fish. It was full of bones and too small to stop our hunger, but nobody complained. When darkness fell, we curled up together in the boat, trying to keep warm.

The boys were already asleep when I awakened to the sounds of horses' hooves on hard ground and the murmur of voices. On my knees in the boat, I parted the grasses. Dark shapes glided through the trees, and campfires flickered in a clearing. Then tents went up, flapping like ghosts in the darkness.

Slowly, quietly, I shook the boys awake. "Shhh! Soldiers."

Chapter Twelve

The Soldier

SAMMY DREW IN HIS BREATH. "Ours or theirs?"

"I can't tell."

"They won't see us here," Neddie whispered. "We'll just wait till they break camp in the morning."

Sammy's hand found mine in the dark. "Don't worry," he whispered. "I still have my knife."

"Be still now. No more talking."

At first light, the camp came to life. Smoke from cooking fires curled into the trees. Soon the air smelled of coffee and frying bacon. A bugle sounded. Men in army uniforms moved through the trees, laughing and shouting as the horses were saddled. A Union flag fluttered in the breeze.

With pounding heart, I crouched in the boat, watching. Sammy blinked awake. Covering his mouth with my palm, I whispered, "Yankees."

We woke Neddie and watched the soldiers pack up their tents. When the tide came in, it lifted our boat from its hiding place. Lying so still made our arms and legs ache, but we dared not leave the safety of our boat.

After a while, the woods grew so quiet we began to hope the soldiers had gone. Then the steady beat of horses' hooves sounded across the water.

"Duck!" Neddie cried. "They're coming this way!"

The soldiers thundered past so close that we could see the shine of their boots and the gleam of their rattling sabers. Dirt from the horses' hooves rained down on us. Neddie's fingers dug into my leg. Sammy crouched beside me, so close I could feel his heartbeat.

Our boat rode higher on the water, turning and bobbing on its tether. I felt faint. What would become of us if we were discovered?

Then the sounds faded away. For a moment we couldn't speak. Neddie slumped in the boat. "Now what?"

"I'm not sure. Maybe we should leave the boat here and try to walk to the railroad."

"It might be faster, but I don't know. With all those soldiers around, it's probably safer out here."

"If only I knew what was on the other side of those trees . . ."

"You can't go out there. What if the Yankees come back?"

I caught his chin in my hand the way Kit did when she wanted his attention. "Listen. The Yankees are getting closer to Papa every minute. We don't have much time."

"You don't know that for sure," he said. "Nobody knows what the Yankees will do. And we don't even know where Papa is. He could be in Timbuktu for all we know."

"John Chapin said the Yankees were heading south. But those soldiers were riding north."

"I give up. What are you thinking?"

"If I can tell where the railroad is, we'll know whether to walk or stay with the boat."

"I guess you could get pretty close if you kept near the bank," Neddie said. "But don't go past that first stand of trees, Susanna. No matter what."

"I won't. Wait here."

"Here," Sammy said. "You might need this." He handed me his knife.

Slipping it into my pocket, I stepped from the boat and picked my way through the vines and grasses, skirting the water till I reached the Yankees' camp. The fires were still smoking. Wet coffee grounds and horse droppings were everywhere. The ground was full of holes where the tent stakes had been.

At a sudden movement in the shadows, I stopped, listening. Two fat blue jays fluttered in the trees. I walked on.

"You there!" a voice commanded. "Halt!"

Out of the shadows stepped a Yankee soldier.

Too frightened to scream or run, I thought only of Neddie and Sammy hiding in the boat.

The soldier dashed across the clearing and threw himself on me, knocking me to the ground, stopping my breath. He lunged for my wrists and I scratched at his face. We rolled over and over in the damp earth, the horse droppings smearing my hair and clothes. Sharp pine needles dug into my skin. I tried to reach into my pocket for Sammy's knife, but the soldier's weight made it impossible.

Summoning my last bit of strength, I wrenched one arm free and struck his face.

"Unhh!" He pulled away but held fast my wrists. Then, for the first time, we really looked at each other, and I saw that he was hardly more than a boy.

"Saints *above*!" he cried. "You're a girl!"

He got to his feet and stood over me, his hand on his pistol. "You can get up now, but if you run I'll shoot. Do you understand?"

Without speaking a single word, I stood up and brushed at the dirt and dung on my clothes. My hands were shaking, but my insides felt frozen.

"What are you doing out here?" he asked.

"It's none of your concern."

"Yes it is. My unit is on patrol in these parts. It's my duty to question anybody we find out here."

"Your duty? Why don't you go back up North where you belong and leave us alone?"

"Believe me, if I had a choice I'd leave right this minute and never come back."

His words left me staring in astonishment. Since the beginning of the war, we'd heard little else but that the Yankees were lawless and vile, an enormous tide of evil bent on destroying everything. Yet here stood an ordinary boy who seemed as weary of the war as I was.

He said, "But, I'm here now, so I have to ask you. Where are you from, and what are you doing here?"

"I was fishing."

"Fishing? All by yourself?"

"Yes."

"I don't believe you. We're miles from the nearest town."

I made no reply. The less I said, the safer Neddie and Sammy would be.

"All right then," he said. "Where's your boat?"

"I walked."

"You walked. All that way."

I stared at him, awaiting my moment to escape.

Birds sang in the trees. From somewhere deep in the woods, a horse was blowing and pawing the ground.

"Look," he said at last. "I know how you feel—"

"No you don't. No one chased you out of your home with little more than the clothes on your back. Why can't you leave us alone? All we want is our freedom."

"Your freedom? You people are fighting to keep another whole race in slavery. Does that seem fair to you?"

His words so troubled my heart that I couldn't think of a proper answer. Papa always said some people were born to be masters and some were born to be slaves. It had been the same for hundreds of years and never had I questioned the rightness of it. Now the Yankees wanted to change everything. "My papa says we'll never have peace as long as you insist on telling us what to do."

"Whether you or your *papa* like it or not," he said, "slavery is over. It's stupid to keep sending boys out to die defending it."

I looked past his shoulder, wondering whether I dared risk running. But he still had one hand on his weapon, enjoying the chance to lecture me. Hooking one thumb into his braces, he went on. "What this whole thing boils down to is pride. Maybe someday you'll see how too much pride can make almost anything seem worth dying for."

"Pride? You don't know anything about anything."

"Maybe I don't. But you seem to know a lot about everything." For the first time, he looked uncertain. "Maybe I should take you to my captain. How do I know you're not a Rebel spy?"

A new wave of fear washed over me. Sammy's knife was a tantalizing weight in my pocket, but unless I could distract the soldier long enough to open the blade, it was useless. "I told you. I was fishing. That's all."

I tried to think of a way to escape without leading him to Sammy and Neddie, but my mind wouldn't work. My heart was beating too fast. Every breath felt like broken glass pressing inside my chest.

At last he said, "I don't believe a word of your cockeyed story. But you know something? I don't care anymore. As near as I can tell, the only thing this war has done so far is tear families apart."

At least we agreed on that. If not for the war, Papa never would have left us.

The soldier's expression changed as if he'd suddenly been transported to another place. "If it weren't for this war, you know what I'd be doing right now? I'd be driving the cows home of an evening, and helping Pa in the apple orchard, and walking Laurie Ann Rush home from church on Sunday. What am I doing in the middle of a swamp, beating up on a *girl*? Go on. Get. Before the captain comes back."

And he turned and walked away.

I raced through the woods and along the bank to the boat. My legs felt heavy, as if I were running under water or in a dream. At last I saw my brothers' heads poking through the grass.

"Holy smokes!" Neddie cried. "What happened to you?"

"Phe-ew!" Sammy held his nose. "You stink worse than an outhouse in August!"

I dropped to my knees and was sick in the tall grass. I washed my face, and they helped me back into the boat.

"Are you all right?" Neddie asked. "You were gone forever! What did you find out? Did you see the railroad?"

I told them about my encounter with the soldier and how he had let me go.

"You should have killed him," Sammy said, his expression fierce. "You should have stabbed him with my knife. That would teach them to mess with us."

"Did you see the railroad?" Neddie asked again. "Are we close?"

"I didn't get that far."

"All that for nothing. And look at how much time we've wasted."

His voice sounded high and far away. I touched his forehead. "Oh, Neddie! You're sick again! You're burning up with fever!"

He shook off my hand. "I'm all right. Let's get going."

Then he crumpled onto the bottom of the boat. Sammy took off his shirt and made a pillow. I was nearly overcome with despair. Coosawhatchie still lay many miles distant, and we were without food or medicine. Why hadn't Neddie stayed behind? Why hadn't I made him go back?

Anger and fear rose up inside me, but I couldn't give up. Not when Papa was in so much danger. "Let's follow the creek a while longer," I said. "I still feel safer on the water."

For another two days, we wound through the marshes and along the placid rivers with no food and very little sleep. Neddie shivered and burned day and night, but there was nothing I could do to comfort him. Near evening of the second day, the water narrowed to a brown trickle. Unlocking the oars, we pushed through a carpet of thick grasses that stretched as far as we could see until at last we scraped bottom. Ahead of us lay solid land, flat and brown and ringed with trees.

We left the boat and started walking into the sun, Neddie leaning on Sammy and me.

"I'm hungry," Sammy complained. "And my feet hurt."

Bitterness welled in my throat. "You should have thought of that before you came. I didn't ask you to follow me, so you can just stop whining."

"Don't scold him," Neddie said wearily. "He's just a little boy."

"I am not," Sammy said. "I'll be eight next summer."

"Both of you, hush. I'm too tired to listen to your arguing." I bent to roll up my trouser legs again. And then from far away came the sound of a train whistle.

"We did it, Susanna!" Neddie exclaimed. "We actually did it!"

We waded a narrow creek and scrambled up the other side just as the train sped past, its whistle screaming, sparks flying out from the great black wheels. Hot cinders rained down on us. Covered in mud and sweat and ashes, unmindful of the deafening roar of the engine, we held on to each other, laughing. We had found the railroad.

We followed the rails until Neddie folded himself onto the ground. "I'm too tired. I have to rest."

We fashioned a container from Neddie's hat and Sammy ran back to the creek for water. We drank it down, trying not to think about how alone we were. Overcome with hunger and weariness, we lay in a mossy clearing beside the tracks. Though I was worried about Neddie, now that we'd found the railroad, I felt more hopeful. Once we reached Coosawhatchie, once General Lee found Papa, everything that had gone wrong in our world would come right again.

But when morning came, all my confidence vanished. Neddie was worse. His lips were puffy and cracked and spotted with blood, his breathing quick and shallow. Sammy looked terrified.

"What are we going to do, Susanna?" he asked.

"I don't know! Why must you ask so many questions? Why must I always be responsible for everything?"

"I thought you knew about medicines. I thought you could make Neddie well."

"Well, maybe I can't. Maybe I don't know anything. And there's no medicine here anyway. Look around you, Sammy. There's nothing and no one to help us!"

"What will you do then? Sit here and watch Neddie die?"

"How can you say such a dreadful thing? Leave me alone!"

I turned and ran until my chest hurt and my legs would carry me no farther. Then the tears came and wouldn't stop.

I was hungry and dirty and afraid, and there didn't seem to be any end to it. Worst of all was the certain knowledge that I would never become a doctor. The burdens were too great and there was too much to learn. The truth of it was like ashes in my mouth.

When at last my tears stopped, I sat up, gathering my thoughts. I might never be a real doctor, but something had to be done for Neddie. I remembered the time Papa and I visited an old fisherman on Petty's Island. Though he was very sick, he refused all of Papa's medicines. He said the things that grew in the woods were better. Things like willow bark, mayapple, and sassafras. And figwort. He had a glass bottle full of the fuzzy dried leaves. Papa had brewed them into a tea for his fever.

Beneath my feet the forest floor was thick with leaves and moss and curling vines. Perhaps there was figwort, too. Flannel plant was what Papa called it when we chanced upon it at home.

"Susanna?" Sammy came through the bushes, his face red and blotchy with tears, his shirt in tatters. "Are you ever coming back?"

"Of course I am, you little goose. Go back and stay with Neddie."

"What are you doing?"

"Looking for plants to make medicine."

His troubled face lit up. "See? I knew you'd think of something. You're a genuine genius."

"It might not work, but it's all we have."

It took a long time to gather the figwort, but at last I collected enough for tea. Sammy went for water and we boiled the leaves a few at a time, in Neddie's tin box till the water turned dark, then we helped Neddie drink it down.

"He'll be better tomorrow," Sammy said. "Then we'll go get Papa."

"We can't wait till tomorrow," Neddie said. "You have to go on, Susanna."

The thought of leaving him in the wilderness was troubling, but our circumstances required action. The next train might not come along for hours. Days. And even if it did, it wouldn't stop way out here, miles from a station. Meanwhile, the Yankee soldiers were closing in on Coosawhatchie.

"You have to find Papa," Neddie said.

"Will you be all right?"

"Sammy will stay with me. When you get to Coosawhatchie, you can send someone to get us."

"Oh, Neddie! I don't like this one bit."

"Me either. But it's the only way."

"Don't worry," Sammy said. "I won't let anything happen to him."

"I know you won't. I'm counting on you."

"You won't forget us, will you?" Sammy asked.

"Of course not, you little goose. How could I forget you?" Neddie said, "You'd better get going."

"I'll send someone for you right away," I promised.

Setting off down the track, I kept a steady pace, looking for places to hide should the Yankees reappear. The track curved through the shadowy trees and over wooden bridges that echoed with my footsteps. The only other sound was the wind rustling in the trees.

For hours there was no sign of town or station. Worry buzzed like a troublesome mosquito inside my head. What if I'd made a grievous mistake and gone in the wrong direction after all? Then I came to a bend in the track and there was a wooden sign nailed to the trunk of a tree.

COOSAWHATCHIE.

Chapter Thirteen

The General

COOSAWHATCHIE WAS JUST AS the man with the cigar had described it. Besides a few houses and a hotel, there was nothing except the train station and the fort, which was a square brown building with a long, low porch across the front.

When I walked into the yard, exhausted, thirsty, and covered with dirt, a soldier who had been leaning against the wall suddenly stood up straight and squinted at me. "Lordy mercy! Where'd you come from?"

"Charleston," I said. "I've come to see General Lee."

"Is that so?" He stared at me so intently that my face grew warm. Truly, I must have been the most disagreeable-looking creature he'd seen in a long time. He said, "The general's HQ is in a house down the road. But he's over to the hospital now. Why don't you tell me your business, and I'll pass the word as soon as he's free."

"The hospital? There's a hospital here?"

"Yep. In the old cotton warehouse out past Anson Road."

"Would you know if my father's there? Dr. William Simons?"

"Afraid not. I just come here yesterday myself."

"Where is it? How do I get there?"

He pointed. "Down thataway past the depot, then off to your left, about a quarter mile. You can't miss it. But it surely ain't no place for a girl, even if she is wearing britches!"

I hurried down the road, past a row of low wooden buildings, the hotel, and the depot, then left, past a meadow where horses grazed, until at last I came to the warehouse.

Inside was a scene so horrifying that for a moment I could scarcely take it in. Rows and rows of the sick and wounded lay on cots in one big room. High in the rafters an oil lamp swayed, its flickering light making dark shadows on the wall. The smells of blood and vomit filled the air. Never before had I seen anything so hopeless and so unspeakably sad.

"Papa?"

There was no answer. Still as statues in a graveyard, the soldiers lay there, too sick to bother with their filthy bandages or the clouds of flies swarming about their heads. A sudden remembrance of Darcy Miles brought me to tears. Had he died this way, alone in a putrid room with no one to comfort him or hear his last words?

Something beside me rattled and a hand came up to touch mine.

"Please," said the soldier on the cot. "Some water."

I looked around, hoping to see the general, hoping to find someone to help these poor men.

"Please," he said again. "It's by the door."

I couldn't bear to let him want for something so simple as a drink of water. I filled the dipper from a wooden bucket and held his shoulders while he drank it down. He lay back and closed his eyes.

Then another voice said, "Please, miss. Over here."

I had to find the general and get help for Neddie. But something pulled at me, wouldn't let me turn away. I knelt beside the soldier's cot. The sour smells of vomit and tobacco juice made my stomach churn. Flies swarmed around my head and settled on my sleeve.

"Thank God," the soldier said. "I prayed for an angel, and He's sent one."

My heart shattered like a piece of glass. "What is it? Tell me how to help you."

"Nothing can help me, miss. They say I've got the camp fever."

"You mustn't talk that way! You will get well. They'll bring you some medicine and you'll go back to your family."

"No. I don't reckon so." He was so weak I had to lean closer to hear his next words. "Got a letter yesterday, but . . . too sick to read it. Would you . . . ?"

From beneath his blanket, he produced a thin letter, mud-spattered and wrinkled.

"'December 6, 1861,'" I read. "'My Darling Jim: Yesterday

brought word that you were taken by train to the hospital in someplace I can't even spell. But they say it's not too far from Charleston. They told me you were only sick, and not wounded, so I suppose we should be thankful for that. I was terribly upset when they said you'd traveled in a railroad car used for shipping animals. How dreadful that must have been for you. The children are fine. Wade is learning his letters and the baby smiled at me yesterday. We all miss you so much and pray you'll be home by Christmas. We . . .'"

He took a long, hard breath. His lips had turned blue, a certain sign he needed more air. While I was looking about for something to use as a fan, a voice behind me said, "Here. Take this."

A soldier on crutches handed me a newspaper. I folded it and fanned my patient. His chest heaved as he struggled for breath. Soaking the corner of his blanket, I squeezed some water onto his lips.

"He should sit up," I said to my assistant. "Will you help me lift him?"

Together we placed a folded blanket at his back, and in a few minutes his breathing eased. I stood up to leave.

"That was a fine thing you did, miss." The soldier on crutches leaned against the wall. "Most girls wouldn't dare set foot in a place like this, but you act like it comes to you natural." He looked down at his friend. "He seems some better. You were a great comfort to him, reading his letter and all."

All around the shadowed room, soldiers were sitting up on their cots, watching me, their eyes full of hope and pain. Only a few months before, they'd left their homes strong in body and spirit. But the war had transformed them into old men, sick and sad. Now they were deathly pale, their skin loose and wrinkled, like bits of crumpled linen.

I'd been wrong about becoming a doctor. It was something I had to do, even if it was difficult and discouraging. Elias was right—some things were too important ever to give up. Despite the horrors of that awful place, a kind of peacefulness filled my troubled heart. I returned the soldier's newspaper.

"What are you doing in this place?" he asked.

"I'm looking for General Lee so that he can help me find my father. And I have to get help for my brother right away. He's awfully sick and there's only our baby brother to look after him."

"If you're wanting the general, you should try his headquarters. It's the white house at the end of Main Street. Near the depot."

"But the soldier at the fort told me to come here."

"The general was here a while ago. He comes by every day to visit the men. By now he's more than likely back at HQ. But he's an awful busy man. I wouldn't get my heart set on seeing him if I were you."

"I must see him, no matter what."

"Good luck then. I hope you find your pa."

Returning to town, I found my way to General Lee's office. Two sentries were in the yard, too busy discussing the horse one was riding to notice me. I pushed open the gate and went up the steps, dusting off my trousers and tucking my falling-down hair behind my ears. Then, standing very straight, I knocked at the door.

In a moment, it opened and there stood the general, looking exactly like his picture from the newspaper. It would be impossible to say which of us was more astonished. We took each other's measure, and though I looked an awful fright, he said kindly, "What is it, precious child?"

Now that the moment so long awaited had finally arrived, I found it hard to speak. But at last I managed to say, "I'm Susanna Simons."

"Simons! You're William Simons's daughter!"

"Yes! Is he here? Is he all right?"

"Please," General Lee said. "Come in and sit down."

We went into a room with a desk, a chair, and a low stool pulled close to the fire. We sat down, he behind his desk, I on the stool beside him. "What about my papa? Do you know where he is?"

General Lee stroked his snowy beard. "A week ago, I got word he was down in Georgia and on his way home to Charleston."

"Then he must have received my message. Only now I'm here, and Neddie is sick, and oh! what a mess I've made."

"Slow down, child. Who's Neddie?"

"My brother. He's sick with fever and I left him beside the railroad track. There's only Sammy to help and he's not eight years old."

"Which direction?" The general's voice was so soothing and reasonable, his dark eyes so kind that I began to feel calm.

"A few miles east of here, on the other side of a bridge. We came from Charleston in the boat and then . . ."

"Wait a minute," he said. "Do I understand you correctly? You came all this way in a boat, with two small boys in tow?"

"Not on purpose. The boys I mean. I planned to come alone, but they followed me."

"I see. Then we must send for them at once. It'll be dark soon. Wait right here."

Leaving me to the warmth of the fire, he went to another room and spoke to a soldier. When he came back, he listened while I described our escape from Oakwood and my efforts to find him at the train station the night of the fire. "But you left before I could speak to you."

He frowned. "I meant to take the evening train, but I was delayed. I was still at the Mills House when the fire broke out. A tragic affair."

"But I saw some soldiers at the station, talking to a general."

"That must have been General Ripley. Dear child, I'm sorry I wasn't there when you needed me. Your father has been of great service to me. Tell me, did your house escape the fire?"

"No. We lost everything, and we need our father back."

And then I related the cigar man's story about the Yankees and their plan to destroy the railroad, and how I'd come to find Papa and bring him home.

The general didn't laugh at me at all. He put another log on the fire and said, "What a brave child you are! You must be hungry. I've asked my aide to bring us some tea."

When the food came, it was only bread and jam and a bit of meat, but after traveling so long without anything to eat, I could have devoured it all, including the napkins and the blue china plates. Even in such circumstances, though, Papa would have expected me to behave like a lady. I sipped the tea and nibbled on the bread.

General Lee said, "Now. About your father. We'll send word right away. You and your brothers will wait here until he comes for you."

Then everything caught up with me and I began to weep. Kneeling beside me, the general took my head onto his shoulder. "There now," he said. "Everything is all right."

"I'm sorry. Now your jacket is all wet."

"No need to apologize." His smile was like Papa's, gentle and kind. "I have four daughters at home. I'm certainly no stranger to tears."

We heard a commotion in the yard. A soldier kicked open the door and came in with Neddie in his arms,

Sammy at his heels. "What should I do with him, sir? He's in a bad way."

"Lay him by the fire," General Lee said. "He's better off here than out at that hospital with the men."

"We made it, Princess Susanna," Neddie said. Then he fell asleep.

Sammy stood there, wonder-struck. "Are you really General Lee?"

"I am indeed," the general said, smiling.

"Do you know where my papa is?"

"Not exactly. But I'm looking for him." He knelt beside Sammy. "What's your name?"

"Sammy. I mean, Samuel."

"It's a very great honor to meet you, sir," the general said gravely.

Sammy's face lit up. He held out his hand to me. "See this? I'm never washing it in a million years, 'cause the general shook it."

General Lee laughed and his eyes twinkled. "I wouldn't advise that, Samuel. Are you hungry?"

"Yes sir."

After sending for more food for Sammy, the general said, "I'm going to arrange a place for you at the hotel. It's not as fine as the Mills House, but it's clean. And you all must rest."

He left us there in front of the fire with an enormous pot of tea, another tray of bread and butter and jam, and a soldier to watch over Neddie.

When he returned, he spoke to his aide, and soon Neddie was bundled onto a stretcher and carried down the street to the hotel. It was not nearly as elegant as the places we'd stayed on our travels with Papa, but it was safe and dry. The innkeeper, a kind-faced woman named Mrs. Burke, promised to look after us.

Because there were so many soldiers about, the only vacant room was a small, windowless one off the kitchen. It smelled of cooking grease and tobacco, but we were so tired after our frightful journey that it seemed fine as a palace.

Neddie and Sammy shared the bed and I slept on a pile of blankets on the floor. While we rested, Mrs. Burke washed our clothes, and when we woke, she heated water and we took turns bathing in a copper tub.

For five days we waited without any news of Papa, and my worry grew with each one that passed. Every day I mixed molasses and sulfur for Neddie. Though he was improving, he slept most of the time.

Then on the sixth day, while Neddie slept under Mrs. Burke's watchful eye, Sammy and I took tea with the general. He told us about each of his children, and about his wife, Mary, and their house in Virginia called Arlington. He said he'd just bought a horse called Greenbrier, but that he planned to name him Traveller. We had finished our bread and jam and were listening to more of the general's stories when we heard voices in the yard and two soldiers came in.

One said, "General Lee, Sir?"

"What is it?"

"You're needed at the hospital. We found a man lying out on Anson Road and he insists on seeing you. Says his name is Simons."

Chapter Fourteen

The Homecoming

SAMMY JUMPED UP, sending the teapot tumbling to the floor. "It's Papa!"

"Is he all right?" I felt like laughing and crying all at once.

"Can't say, miss," said the soldier. "He fainted dead away before we got him to the hospital. He just kept asking for the general."

Then the other soldier said, "You must be the ones everybody is talking about. They say you came down the backcountry in a rowboat. Is it true?"

"Every bit of it," Sammy said. "My sister is a genuine genius."

General Lee said, "You children will come with me and Lieutenant Lowell. Neddie will be fine at the hotel until we get this sorted out."

Sammy danced around the room. "Won't he be surprised when he wakes up and sees Papa?"

"I expect so, Samuel," the general said, "but no more

surprised than your father will be to find his children so far from home."

The horses were brought into the yard. Lieutenant Lowell helped me into his saddle. Sammy rode with General Lee on Traveller. On horseback the journey was short, but I thought my heart would burst before we reached the hospital, wondering whether it truly was Papa who'd been found on the road.

We went in, and the lieutenant led us past the rows of sick soldiers to a cot in the corner where a grizzled man, pale as death, lay sleeping.

"Oh, Papa!" I bent over the bed. "Is it really you?"

His eyes fluttered open. Then he smiled. "Susanna."

My heart danced inside my chest. I felt light as a thistle.

Sammy said, "You wouldn't come home, Papa, and it's almost Christmas. So we came to get you."

"Samuel? What are you children doing here?"

"We'll explain later," General Lee said. "How are you, sir? Are you terribly ill?"

"I'll survive, General." Papa sat up. "It was hunger that made me faint. I ran into some Federals on the way back from Georgia. I must say they were not very hospitable. Stole my horse and all my provisions. I haven't eaten in days."

"Federals?" the lieutenant asked. "You were captured?"

"Just outside Savannah. Took me a while to escape."

"They must be grievously disappointed at having lost a prisoner," the general said, his expression merry. "The last I heard, you were on your way home. What happened to bring you back here?"

"I heard some talk I thought you should know about," Papa said. "It may not be true, but I decided to come here first and tell you, just in case."

"Come on." The lieutenant motioned to Sammy and me. "Let's go outside for a while."

Papa had learned something important about the Yankees. Something that had to be kept secret. We went outside with Lieutenant Lowell, who lifted Sammy onto his horse again. Waiting beneath the bare trees, I wondered what would happen next. If the Yankees had truly taken over our island, where would we go?

The hospital door creaked open and out came Papa. His dear face lit up as if he were seeing me for the first time. "Susanna. What an extraordinary costume!"

"She borrowed the pants from Mr. Willis," Sammy said, dismounting the horse. "She looks like a boy."

For once, Papa seemed unconcerned with my appearance. Despite his weakened condition, he lifted me up and kissed my forehead, and it was more wonderful than in my dreams. Then he embraced Sammy, and we all talked and laughed at once, tears streaming down our faces.

"Where's Ned?" Papa asked.

We told him about our journey, and the Yankee soldiers, and how Neddie had gotten sick.

"Susanna made medicine out of some weeds and I stayed with him till our soldiers came," Sammy said. He was clinging to Papa like a lizard to a log. "I was a big help."

"I imagine so." Papa turned to me. "Is he all right?"

"He's sleeping. We've been giving him a tonic."

"Good. What did you use in the woods?"

"Figwort."

He rubbed his stubbled face. "While I was captured, I thought of you, my dear. I knew that if something happened and I never came home, you'd carry on my work. It was a great comfort to me."

General Lee came outside. "I'll send a carriage to take you to the hotel. You're long overdue for a decent meal and a good rest."

"Thank you, General," Papa said.

General Lee shook Papa's hand. "The Confederacy owes you a great debt, William. You've served with boldness and intelligence. I only pray God will bless our efforts and bring a swift end to this war. In the meantime, I suggest you take these precious children home."

"I'll send you a report on the hospitals as soon as I can," Papa said.

And just like that, because Papa was never really in the army, it was over.

The carriage came to take us to the hotel. Papa woke Neddie, and the sight of our father was the best medicine of all. Mrs. Burke made tea, and General Lee sent over a supper of beef and corn bread and ginger cake. Neddie talked and talked, until at last Papa asked for more blankets and we slept ever so peacefully at long last.

The next morning, we boarded the train for Charleston. Someone called out, "Make way for sick soldiers!" One of them recognized Papa and saluted. Papa saluted back, even though he wasn't a real officer.

We gave them our seats and moved to the back of the train. Papa said it would be best not to discuss his troubles down in Georgia, in case there were Yankee spies about. So we told him more about the fire and how Miss Hastings had taken us in. I told him about the dance.

"You went to a dance? Voluntarily? I can scarcely believe it."

"She only went to please Miss Hastings," Neddie said. "But I heard she was the prettiest girl there."

Of course, Neddie had heard no such thing. That was just his way.

Sammy told Papa all about Jeremy, and that it was Jeremy's boat that got us to Coosawhatchie.

Papa said, "I suppose we owe your friend a new boat, Sammy."

"He won't care," Sammy said. "He's going to live in Atlanta. Besides, he'll know we took it for a good cause."

A good cause. Was this war truly a good cause or only a futile effort to save our pride, as the Yankee soldier had said? I thought about Darcy, about Elias and his freedom dream, and about all those poor, sick soldiers in the Coosawhatchie hospital. However hard I tried, it was impossible to sort out my feelings. They were a hopeless jumble, like the numbers in Papa's account books.

While Neddie slept in the curve of Papa's arm, Sammy recounted the night of the fire and how our house on

Meeting Street had burned. "Now that you're back we can go home to Oakwood, can't we?" he asked. "You won't let the Yankees onto Terrapin Island, will you, Papa?"

A look of profound sadness crept onto Papa's face. He shook Neddie, saying quietly, "Wake up, son."

Neddie sat up and rubbed his eyes. "What is it?"

"There's something you must know. Just before I was captured, I rode back to Oakwood. I'd heard about Port Royal, and I had to be sure you were safe."

"Is it bad?"

"Worse than I'd imagined," Papa said. "The house is still standing, but it might as well not be. The Yankees ripped all the doors off their hinges, shot out every window in the place. The furniture is full of bullet holes. All your mother's things are gone."

"What about her portrait?" I asked.

"Slashed to ribbons. It made me ill to look at it."

Neddie clenched his fists. "Oh, I hope this war does go on, till I'm old enough to fight! I hope I have a chance to kill those cowardly devils. I could kill them with my bare hands!"

"Isn't there *anything* left?" I asked.

"Not a solitary thing. They stole what little cotton had been picked. I hear they're planning to sell it and send the money up North. Such bitter irony, using the sale of our own crop to pay for the war against us." He sighed. "Livestock's all gone, too. Shot dead in their tracks."

"Oh, Papa. Not Cherokee!"

"I'm sorry, my dear. I know how much you loved him."

I squeezed my eyes shut against hot, bitter tears. I felt so helpless against the tide of events sweeping over us. We had lost more than our houses. More than tables and chairs and paintings. All our cherished ideals, everything we thought to be good and right and true had perished, too, and all my wishing and hoping would never bring it back.

"Don't cry," Sammy said, patting my shoulder. "When I get the money, I'll buy you another horse. You just wait and see if I don't."

Papa kissed my cheek. "I wish I could have spared you this sorrow, but it's better to know the truth than to harbor false hope."

The train rocked on, swaying around the long curves, and I slept against Papa's shoulder until we reached the station.

We arrived in early afternoon, beneath a cold gray sky. First we went to Miss Hastings's house. After she kissed us all, and gave us some tea, and wept a little, Papa explained everything.

When he finished, she said, "Oh, my dears! I'm so glad you're all right. You gave me quite a turn, coming up missing like that."

"We're sorry," Sammy said. "It was all Susanna's idea."

"Oh! Blame me, Sammy!"

"Well, it was!"

"Nobody asked you to come along."

"But you wouldn't have made it without me," he said. "I brought you good luck, see?"

And he pulled out the rabbit's foot he'd planned to give Papa the day Papa left Oakwood. "I had it with me the whole time. And that's why we didn't drown in the river and why we found the railroad just in time."

"Somehow, I think it had more to do with common sense and uncommon courage," Miss Hastings said. "But I hope you won't ever again do anything so dangerous."

"You may depend on that," Papa said. "From now on, I'm not letting these three out of my sight."

Then Papa wanted to see what was left of our house. The street was deserted and quiet as stone. A solitary crow flapped onto the burned-out chimney top. We waited while Papa sifted through the ashes.

"Susanna!" Papa stirred the ashes. There beneath the gray was the red-and-gold gleam of my mother's bracelet. Lifting it up, he said, "It's not even broken."

He fastened it onto my wrist. "Let's walk down to the harbor. I've missed it."

With Sammy atop Papa's shoulders, we continued on past the burned-out houses and down to the battery, watching the seabirds wheeling overhead and the tide peeling away from the clean-washed shore. Standing there with Papa, I understood something.

There are some things in life you can't do anything about. Like the wind and the tide, they can only be accepted. A tadpole turns into a frog, a caterpillar becomes a butterfly, and nothing is the same ever again. Because of the war, we were changed forever. We could never go back to the way it was before.

But Papa was home, and we would wake up safe in the morning.

Author's Note

READERS OFTEN ASK which parts of a story are fiction and which are true. Terrapin Island and Oakwood Plantation are fictional, but they are based upon actual places in the South Carolina low country. Except for General Lee, all the characters are fictional as well. I was inspired to create the character of Susanna Simons after reading about the real-life Eliza Lucas who, in 1739, was left in charge of three South Carolina plantations at age fifteen while her father was away serving in the British army.

While the setting and characters are imaginary, the invasion by Federal troops at Port Royal and the great fire that destroyed much of Charleston actually happened much as I've described them. As terrible as these events were, they were only the beginning of trouble.

For many years before the War Between the States actually began, planters all across the South worried that Congress would outlaw slavery. Such action would mean the loss of their labor supply, and therefore the loss of their way of life. In South Carolina, men such as Robert Barnwell Rhett and John C. Calhoun spoke in favor of the right of each state to decide the issue and supported the idea of secession. Others, such as Benjamin Perry and James Petigru, fought to preserve the union. In 1860 Abraham Lincoln was elected President of the United States and leaders in South Carolina decided the time for secession had come. The legislature called a convention.

The delegates first met in Columbia on December 17, 1860. But a smallpox epidemic forced them out of the city. They moved to Charleston, and three days later all 169 delegates voted to leave the Union.

The people were jubilant, crowding into the streets wearing secession bonnets and waving banners. Cannons boomed, and the bells of St. Michael's church rang wildly. Down came the United States flag and up went the Palmetto flag. Celebratory fires burned all over town.

Four months later, in April of 1861, the first shots of the war thundered over Fort Sumter in Charleston harbor. In the early-morning hours, people raced to their rooftops to cheer the start of what they thought would surely be a short and decisive war. They could not know then that they were witnessing the beginning of the most devastating event in our nation's history.

That autumn, a fleet of Union warships left New York for Port Royal. On November 7, 1861, exactly one year from the day of President Lincoln's election, Federal troops took the harbor.

Leaving behind most of their belongings, families living on the Sea Islands fled to safety. General Robert E. Lee, who had been dispatched to Charleston to supervise harbor defenses, moved to Coosawhatchie, a small town on the Charleston & Savannah Railroad line.

Despite the events at Port Royal, South Carolinians still hoped for a swift end to the war. Ten other states had seceded and a new Confederate government had been formed. Confederate forces had won a battle at Manassas (Bull Run) the previous July. And many Southerners still hoped England would join the war in order to protect the cotton trade. But it was not to be.

The fighting lasted for four long years. By the time General Lee surrendered his Confederate army to General Ulysses S. Grant, more than 600,000 men had died. Nearly every family in the South had lost a father, husband, son, or brother. Explosions, fires, and years of near-constant bombardment left the city of Charleston, so long noted for its beauty and grace, in ruins.

But her people, refusing defeat, rebuilt their beautiful city. Today, quiet gardens and graceful houses line the shady streets, looking much as they did in Susanna's day.

The plantations, however, could not be restored. After the war the planters had no money to buy seeds and no workers to tend the fields. The houses that had survived fell into disrepair and eventually disappeared. A few have been preserved, but most are now only memories.

If you visit the Sea Islands today, stand beneath the ancient trees and listen with your heart. There, amid the silent ruins of a time long past, perhaps you will hear the voices of children from long ago rising up like mist on the river, borne homeward on the evening tide.

BESS'S LOG CABIN QUILT

D. Anne Love

0-440-41197-1

On sale now from Yearling Books

"Joe wouldn't leave us here alone," Mama said. "He adores Bess. He would never abandon her. No matter what."

Bess froze. *They were talking about Papa!*

"All I'm saying is, you should think about what you're going to do if he doesn't come back," Mrs. Fairchild said. "How will you manage the orchards, the animals, the gardens, by yourself? Especially now that you're sick?"

"I have Bess," Mama said. "We'll manage if we have to. But Joe will be back, as soon as he can. You'll see."

"I hope you're right, Sarah. But you've made that trip. You know how dangerous it is. Joe could be killed by Indians or starved to death in the desert. For all we know, the whole lot of them could be drowned in the Snake River."

Bess couldn't listen anymore. She dropped her baskets of eggs and berries and ran for the riverbank as fast as she could. She threw herself on the soft moss and cried as if her heart would break. Papa dead? Impossible. He was the bravest and smartest man ever to travel the Oregon Trail. He would come back! He had to! Hot tears seeped from her eyes and wet the front of her dress. Why, oh why hadn't they stayed in Missouri?

After a long time, she went back to the house. Mrs. Fairchild's horse and buggy were gone. Bess gathered up the eggs and berries and went inside. Mama was waiting for her.

"What happened, Bess? Mrs. Fairchild waited and waited for you." She eyed the damp hem of Bess's dress. "Were you playing beside the river again?"

Bess's bottom lip trembled and a single tear rolled down her cheek. "Has Papa left us here for good? Is he dead?"

"Is Papa . . . Come here, honey." Mama opened her arms and Bess fell into them sobbing. Mama rocked her back and forth.

"So you overheard Mrs. Fairchild talking about him, did you?"

Bess nodded. Mama's cotton gown felt smooth against her cheek.

"You know it's not polite to eavesdrop, don't you?"

"I didn't mean to," Bess said, sniffing. "Is it true, Mama, what she said?"

"Of course not. The wagon train has been delayed for some reason, that's all. Remember when we got snowed in halfway through the Blue Mountains?"

Bess nodded.

"We had to wait nearly a week before we could move on," Mama reminded her. "I'll bet that's where Papa is. Snug as a bug in a rug, waiting for the weather to clear."

"You really think so?"

"Yes, I do," Mama said. "And you mustn't worry anymore about it."

Bess swallowed hard. She wanted to believe that Mama was right. But . . .

"Mama, suppose Papa *doesn't* come back? What then?"

But Mama had fallen into a deep sleep, crumpled against the pillows like Bess's old rag doll.

0-440-41290-0

On sale now from Yearling Books

Excerpt from *Dakota Spring* by D. Anne Love

Published by Dell Yearling

an imprint of

Random House Children's Books

a division of Random House, Inc.

1540 Broadway, New York, New York 10036

"I'll tell him," I said.

We heard the train's bell clanging as we rumbled into the station. Suddenly my mouth went dry and my chest felt tight. I had no idea what my grandmother looked like. How would I recognize her?

We watched the passengers come down the steps from the platform. First came two women with babies in their arms, and then two older ladies carrying matching leather suitcases. A farmer in tattered wool pants came next, then a young man wearing wire-rimmed glasses and an overcoat.

"Well," said Mr. McGuffey. "Which one is your grandmother?"

I scanned the empty platform. My throat closed up, and I felt tears sting my eyes. "I guess she didn't come after all," I said. "How could she do this? Pa was counting on her!"

"Could be she missed her train somewhere along the way," said Mr. McGuffey. He patted my shoulder. "Don't you worry now, I'll just go talk to the stationmaster. Maybe we can figure out what happened."

Just then we heard a commotion and turned back to the platform. The stationmaster struggled down the steps carrying two large trunks. Behind him strode a woman in a gray suit, black leather boots, and a feathered hat.

"For heaven's sake, young man, do be careful!" she said to the stationmaster. "That's a matched set of trunks you're carrying, not sacks of cattle feed!"

She stopped on the bottom step and looked around. The moment her gaze met mine, I felt a thrill crawl up my spine. I'd looked into those same black eyes before. They were my mother's eyes.

0-440-41375-3

On sale now from Yearling Books

Excerpt from *My Lone Star Summer* by D. Anne Love

Text copyright © 1996 by D. Anne Love

Published by Dell Yearling

an imprint of

Random House Children's Books

a division of Random House, Inc.

1540 Broadway, New York, New York 10036

The morning after I got to the ranch, I put on a pair of denim shorts and a T-shirt, made a couple of sandwiches, stuffed a couple of cans of cola in my backpack, and rode out to the river. I couldn't wait to find out why B.J. had spent yesterday afternoon in the back of a pickup with some boy instead of meeting me at the airport like she'd promised; why she hadn't answered her phone all night.

I put the cans in the water to keep them cool and climbed onto the smooth end of the elm tree to wait for her. High above me, a mockingbird chattered for a few minutes, then swept away through the trees. I took out my pen to write a note to Mom. Then I saw B.J. coming through the trees toward the river with the boy from the pickup. He wore black shorts and a white T-shirt, and his face was half hidden behind those dumb-looking wraparound sunglasses. Something must have been terribly funny, because they were laughing like two wild hyenas.

B.J. shaded her eyes with one hand and looked up at me. "Jill! Hi!" That was all. We hadn't seen each other in a year, but she was acting as if it had been only minutes instead of twelve whole months.

"Hi," I said. I couldn't believe she was so dressed up. She wore hot-pink shorts with a matching shirt. Her blond hair, which is usually as straight and unruly as mine, curled around her shoulders as if she'd just come from the beauty shop. In place of her usual grubby tennis shoes, she wore new white sandals. Her lips and toenails were painted bright pink. In other words, she looked like a movie star. And I felt as ugly as the bark on the trees. But something else was bothering me. "How come you didn't show up at the airport yesterday? You promised to come with Gran to pick me up."

"That was my fault," the boy said quickly. "I asked her to go with Dad and me to buy lumber, and it took longer than we planned. I'm sorry I made her late."

I shot him a murderous look. I said to B.J., "Where were you last night? I called your house at least ten times, and nobody answered."

The boy raised his hand, as if he were answering a question in school. "My fault again. I invited her to have supper with us."

B.J. shook out her curls. "I wanted to call you when I got home last night, but Mom wouldn't let me. She said it was too late." She smiled at the boy. "Jill, this is Trey Wilborn. His family just bought the old Hallaby place."

"Hullo," the boy said from behind his dark glasses.

"Hi," I mumbled to the toe of my shoe. "What would anybody want that old place for?"

"They're tearing down the old farmhouse and building a brand-new one," B.J. explained. "They'll be moved in by the time school starts, and guess what? Trey's in ninth grade, so he'll go to the same school as me. Isn't that great?"

"Terrific." I slammed my notebook shut. "B.J., are you going to stand there yelling at me all day, or are you coming up here?"

"B.J.?" Trey cut in.

B.J. tossed her curly mane and smiled at Trey. "That was my nickname when I was a kid." She squinted up at me. "I prefer Belinda now, if you don't mind."

"Okay, *Belinda*. Are you coming up here or not?"

"In these clothes? They're brand new. My mom will kill me if I ruin them."

"Well then," I said. "I don't know why you even bothered to come down here if you're just going to stand there hollering at me."

"Why, to say hi and welcome home, Jill."

I could see that I had hurt her feelings, but she deserved it. She'd hurt mine by not showing up at the airport, then by bringing this strange boy to our secret place on the river, and by making me feel so incredibly ugly.

"Besides," she went on, "I wanted you to meet Trey. He's camping out with his family in an RV while they're building the house." She rested her hand on his arm. "I think it would be so cool to camp out all summer."

"Yeah," Trey said.

"Listen," B.J. said to me. "We're going to the Dairy Queen for a Coke. Trey's cousin is taking us in his truck. Want to come along?"

"No thanks. I have to help Gran."

"She'll let you go with us, Jill. Let's go ask her."

"She's not home," I said. "She's out checking on the cattle."

"Oh," B.J. said. "Later, then. Come on, Trey. We don't want Ricky to leave without us." She waved at me and turned back toward the road.

I watched them disappear into the trees and tried to swallow the lump in my throat. I hung around the river a while longer, watching the squirrels. I skipped a few rocks across the water. But without B.J., nothing was fun, and I took the soft drink cans out of the water and rode back to the house.